THE IRON GATE OF J█████████████████
SCRAPED OPEN HAR███████████████████
OUTSIDE IN THE DUSTY GALE WAS LUKE
SKYWALKER.

Two Gammoreans stepped up, blocking his path. Luke
raised his hand and pointed at them. Before they could
draw their weapons, they were clutching their throats,
choking, gasping.

Luke lowered his hand and walked on. The guards did
not follow.

As Luke entered Jabba's court, the level of tumult
dropped.

Luke let Jabba fill his mind completely. 'You will bring
Captain Solo and the Wookiee to me.'

Jabba smiled grimly. 'Your mind powers will not work
with me, boy.'

Luke's expression did not change. 'Nevertheless, I am
taking Captain Solo and his friends. You can either
profit from this or be destroyed.'

Jabba laughed like a lion threatened by a mouse.
'There will be no bargaining, young Jedi. I shall enjoy
watching you die.'

The floor below Luke dropped suddenly away, sending
him crashing into the pit …

RETURN OF THE JEDI
Trade Mark

Starring

Mark   Harrison   Carrie
Hamill   Ford   Fisher

Billy Dee   Anthony
Williams   Daniels
as C-3PO

Directed by   Produced by
Richard Marquand   Howard Kazanjian

Screenplay by   Story by
Lawrence Kasdan and   George Lucas
George Lucas

                                Music by
Executive Producer   John Williams
George Lucas

James Kahn

Return of the Jedi

Futura
Macdonald & Co
London & Sydney

A Futura Book

First full-length edition published in Great Britain in
1983 by Futura Publications

This abridgement published in Great Britain in 1983
by Futura Publications, a Division of Macdonald &
Co (Publishers) Ltd
London & Sydney

ISBN 0 7088 2424 2

Cover art and insert supplied by Lucasfilm Ltd. (LFL.)

Photoset in North Wales by
Derek Doyle & Associates, Mold, Clwyd.
Printed in Great Britain by Hazell, Watson & Viney
Ltd, Aylesbury, Bucks

Futura Publications
A Division of
Macdonald & Co (Publishers) Ltd
Maxwell House
74 Worship Street
London EC2A 2EN

A long time ago, in a galaxy far, far away ...

PROLOGUE

At the edge of the galaxy the Death Star floated in stationary orbit above the green moon Endor, a moon whose mother planet had long since died and disappeared into unknown realms. The Death Star was the Empire's armoured battle station, nearly twice as big as its predecessor, which Rebel forces had destroyed so many years before. It was more than twice as powerful, yet it was only half completed.

Half a steely dark orb, it hung above the green world of Endor, tentacles of unfinished superstructure curling away towards its living companion like the groping legs of a deadly spider.

An Imperial Star Destroyer approached the giant space station at cruising speed. It was massive – a city itself – yet it moved with deliberate grace, like some great sea dragon. It was accompanied by dozens of Twin Ion Engine fighters, black insect-like combat fliers that zipped back and forth around the battleship's perimeter, scouting, sounding, docking, regrouping.

Soundlessly the main bay of the ship opened. There was a brief ignition flash as an Imperial shuttle emerged from the dark of the hold into the darkness of space. It sped towards the half completed Death Star with quiet purpose.

In the cockpit the shuttle captain and his co-pilot

made final readings and monitored descent functions. It was a sequence they had performed a thousand times, yet there was an unusual tension in the air. The captain flipped the transmission switch and spoke into his mouthpiece.

'Command Station, this is ST321. Code Clearance Blue. We've started our approach. Deactivate the security shield.'

Static filtered over the receiver, then the voice of the port controller. 'The security deflector shield will be deactivated when we have confirmation of your code transmission. Stand by.'

Once more silence filled the cockpit. The shuttle captain smiled nervously at his co-pilot and muttered, 'Quick as you can, please. This had better not take long. He's in no mood to wait.'

They refrained from glancing back into the passenger section of the shuttle. The unmistakable sound of the mechanical breathing coming from the shadow filled the cabin with a terrible impatience. In the Death Star below, the shield operator suddenly checked his monitor with alarm. The viewscreen depicted the battle station itself, the moon Endor and a web of energy – the deflector shield, emanating from the green moon and surrounding the Death Star. Only now, the security web was beginning to retract and form a clear channel through which the dot that was the Imperial shuttle sailed towards the massive space station.

The shuttle operator quickly called his control officer, uncertain how to proceed.

'What is it?' the officer demanded.

'That shuttle has a class one security rating.' He tried to hide the fear in his voice.

The officer glanced at the screen for only a moment

before he realized who was on the shuttle. 'Vader,' he muttered.

He strode past the view port where the shuttle could be seen making its final approach, and headed towards the docking bay. 'Inform the commander that Lord Vader's shuttle has arrived,' he ordered the controller.

The shuttle sat quietly, dwarfed by the cavernous reaches of the docking bay. Hundreds of troops assembled in formation, flanking the base of the shuttle ramp. White-armoured Imperial stormtroopers, grey-suited officers, and the elite, red-robed Imperial Guard all snapped to attention as Moff Jerjerrod entered.

Jerjerrod was the Death Star commander. Tall, thin, arrogant, he walked unhurriedly through the ranks of soldiers to the shuttle ramp and waited with respect. One such as this great Dark Lord could not be taken too lightly.

Suddenly the exit hatch of the shuttle opened. Only darkness glowed from the exit at first, then came footsteps and the characteristic electrical breathing. Finally, Darth Vader, Lord of the Sith, emerged.

Vader strode down the ramp and glanced at the assembled troops. He stopped when he came to Jerjerrod. The commander bowed his head and smiled. 'Lord Vader, this is an unexpected pleasure. We are honoured by your presence.'

'We can dispense with the pleasantries, Commander.' Vader's words echoed. 'The Emperor is concerned with your progress. I am here to put you back on schedule.'

Jerjerrod turned pale. This was news he hadn't expected. 'I assure you, Lord Vader, my men are working as fast as they can.'

'Perhaps I can encourage their progress in ways you

have not considered,' Vader growled.

Jerjerrod kept his tone even. 'That won't be necessary, my Lord. I tell you, without question, that this station will be operational as planned.'

'I'm afraid the Emperor does not share your optimism,' Vader snarled.

'I fear he asks the impossible,' the commander suggested.

'Perhaps you would like to explain that to him when he arrives.' Vader's face remained invisible behind its deathly black mask, but the malice was clear in his electronically controlled voice.

Jerjerrod's pallor intensified. 'The Emperor is coming here?'

'Yes, Commander. And he will be displeased if you are still behind schedule when he arrives.' He spoke loudly, his words a threat to all who heard them.

'We shall double our efforts, Lord Vader,' Jerjerrod promised.

Vader lowered his tone again. 'I hope so, Commander, for your sake. The Emperor will tolerate no further delay in the final destruction of the outlaw Rebellion. And we have secret information that the Rebel fleet has gathered all its forces into a single giant armada. The time is at hand when we can crush them without mercy in a single blow.'

For the briefest moment, Vader's breathing quickened, then resumed its measured pace like the rising of a hollow wind.

CHAPTER ONE

Outside the small adobe hut the sandstorm wailed like a beast in agony, refusing to die. Inside, a shrouded figure worked. Before him was a circular device of strange design, wires trailing from it at one end, and symbols etched into its flat surface.

The figure connected the wired end to a tubular smooth handle, pulled through a connector, and locked it in place with another tool. He motioned to a shadow in the corner, and the shadow moved towards him.

'Vrrr-dit dweet?' the little R2 unit questioned timidly when it was just a foot from the shrouded man.

The man motioned the droid nearer still. Artoo-Detoo scooted the last distance, blinking as the man's hand moved towards his domed little head.

The fine sand blew hard over the dunes of Tatooine. The wind seemed to come from everywhere at once, without pattern or meaning.

A road wound across the desert plain. Its nature changed constantly, at one moment obscured by drifts of yellow sand, the next swept clean or distorted by the shimmering air above it. This was the only road to the palace of Jabba the Hutt.

Jabba was the vilest gangster in the galaxy. His minions were scattered across the stars and he had his fingers in smuggling, slave trading, and murder. He was responsible for uncountable atrocities, and his court was a den of unparalleled decay.

'Poot-weet bedooe gung coble deep,' Artoo-Detoo bleeped.

'Of course I'm worried,' See-Threepio fussed. 'Poor Lando Calrissian never returned from this place. Can you imagine what they've done to him?'

The golden droid waded stiffly through a shifting sand hill, then stopped short as Jabba's palace suddenly loomed in the near distance. Artoo nearly bumped into him, quickly skidding to the side of the road.

'Watch where you're going, Artoo.' See-Threepio resumed walking, his little friend rolling along at his side. 'Why couldn't Chewbacca have delivered this message? Whenever there's an impossible mission they turn to us. No one worries about droids.'

At last they reached the gates of the palace. Massive iron doors, taller than Threepio could see, were set in a series of stone and iron walls that formed several cylindrical towers, rising like mountains out of the packed sand.

The two droids looked fearfully round the iron door for signs of life or some sort of signalling device with which to make their presence known. Seeing nothing, Threepio mustered his resolve and softly knocked three times on the thick metal gate. Quickly, he turned round and said to Artoo, 'There doesn't seem to be anyone here. Let's go back and tell Master Luke.'

Suddenly a small hatch opened in the centre of the gate. A spindly mechanical arm popped out. From the end of it, a large electronic eyeball peered at the two droids. The eyeball spoke. 'Tee chuta hhat yudd!'

Threepio pointed to Artoo and then to himself.

'Artoo Detoowha bo Seethreepiosha ey toota odd mischka Jabba du Hutt.'

The eyeball looked quickly from one robot to the other, then retracted through the hatch and slammed it shut.

Threepio turned to leave. 'I don't think they're going to let us in, Artoo. We'd better go.'

At that, there was a horrific grinding screech and the massive iron gate slowly began to rise. The two droids looked into the yawning cavity that faced them. 'Nudd chaa!' the eye's strange voice shrieked at them from the shadows.

Artoo beeped and rolled forward into the gloom. Threepio hesitated then rushed after him. 'Artoo, wait for me,' he scolded. 'You'll get lost.'

The great door slammed behind them with an echoing crash. Haltingly, the two frightened robots moved forward.

They were immediately joined by three large Gamorrean guards, powerful pig-like brutes whose hatred of robots was well-known. The guards ushered the two droids down a dark corridor. As they reached the first half lit hallway, one of them grunted an order. Artoo beeped a nervous question at Threepio.

'You don't want to know,' the golden droid responded nervously. 'Just deliver Master Luke's message and get us out of here quick.'

Before they could take another step, Bib Fortuna, Jabba's inelegant major-domo, approached them. He was a tall humanoid creature, wearing a robe that hid all. Protruding from the back of his skull were two fat tentacles which he wore either draped over his shoulders or hanging down behind him like twin tails. He smiled thinly at the two robots. 'Die wanna wanga.'

Threepio spoke up. 'Die wanna wanaga. We bring a

message to your master, Jabba the Hutt.' Artoo beeped. Threepio nodded, and added, 'A gift too.' He thought about this for a moment and whispered to Artoo, 'What gift?'

Bib held out his hand at Artoo.

'Artoo, give it to him,' Threepio ordered gruffly.

At this, Artoo beeped and tooted defiantly. Threepio smiled apologetically at Bib. 'He says our master's instructions are to give it only to Jabba himself.'

Bib considered for a moment and gestured for them to follow. He led them into the darkness with the three Gamorrean guards lumbering behind them.

See-Threepio and Artoo-Detoo stood at the entrance of the throne room, looking in. 'We're doomed,' Threepio whimpered.

The room was filled, wall to wall, with the dregs of the Universe. Grotesque creatures from the lowest star systems, drunk on spiced liquor – Gamorreans, twisted humans, jawas, all revelling in base pleasures or raucously comparing their evil deeds. And at the front of the room, reclining on a dais that overlooked the rest, was Jabba the Hutt.

Jabba's head was three times human size, perhaps four. His eyes were yellow, reptilian. His skin was like a snake's too, and covered with a fine layer of grease. He had no neck but only a series of chins that expanded finally into a great bloated body. Stunted, almost useless arms sprouted from the upper torso. The sticky fingers of his left hand were wrapped around the smoking end of his water pipe. He had neither hair nor legs. His trunk simply tapered into a long snake tail that stretched along the platform like a tube of yeasty dough. His lipless mouth stretched almost from ear to ear and he drolled continually. He was thoroughly disgusting.

Chained at the neck to him was a sad, pretty dancing girl, a member of Fortuna's species, with two tentacles sprouting from the back of her head and hanging down her bare, muscled back. Her name was Oola. She sat as far away from Jabba as the chain would allow.

Sitting near Jabba's belly was a small monkey-like reptile called Salacious Crumb who caught all the food and ooze that spilled from Jabba's hands or mouth, and ate it with a sickly cackle.

As Fortuna reached the throne, he leaned forward and whispered into the slobbering monarch's ear. Jabba's eyes became slits. Then, with a maniacal laugh, he motioned for the two droids to be brought in.

'Bo Shuda,' the Hutt wheezed then lapsed into a coughing fit. He understood several languages but spoke only Huttese as a point of honour.

The terrified robots scooted forward. 'The message, Artoo, the message,' Threepio urged.

Artoo whistled. A beam of light projected from his head to create a holograph of Luke Skywalker which stood before them on the floor. Quickly the image grew until the young Jedi warrior towered, ten feet tall, over the assembled throng.

'Greetings, Exalted One,' the hologram said to Jabba. 'I am Luke Skywalker, Jedi Knight and friend of Captain Solo. I seek an audience with Your Greatness to bargain for his life.' At this, the entire room burst into laughter which Jabba stopped instantly with a motion of his hand. 'I know that you are powerful, mighty Jabba,' Luke went on, 'and that you are angry with Solo. But I'm sure that we can work out an arrangement to suit both of us. As a token of my goodwill, I present to you a gift – these two droids. Both are hardworking and will serve you well.'

With that, the hologram disappeared.

Threepio wagged his head in despair. 'Oh no, this can't be,' he wailed.

Bib spoke in Huttese. 'Bargain rather than fight? He is no Jedi.'

Jabba laughed and drooled. Still grinning, he rasped at Threepio, 'There will be no bargain. I have no intention of giving up my favourite decoration.' With a hideous chuckle he looked up to the dimly lit alcove above the throne. There, hanging flat against the wall, was the carbonized form of Han Solo, his face and hands emerging from the cold hard slab, like a statue reaching from a sea of stone.

Artoo and Threepio marched dismally through the dank passage, prodded by a Gamorrean guard. Dungeons lined both walls. The cries of anguish which emanated from within echoed off the stone and down the endless catacombs. Periodically a hand or claw or tentacle reached through the bars of a door to grab at the hapless robots.

The door at the end of the corridor opened automatically and the Gamorrean shoved them forward. Their ears were assaulted by defeaning machine sounds, and a continuously shifting haze of steam made visibility short. This was either the boiler room or hell.

An agonized electronic scream like the sound of stripping gears drew their attention to the corner of the room. From out of the mist walked EV-9D9, a thin human-like robot with some disturbingly human appetites. In the dimness behind Ninedenine, Threepio could see the legs being pulled off a droid on a torture rack, while a second droid, hanging upside down, was having red-hot irons applied to its feet.

Nindenine stopped in front of Threepio, raising her pincer hands, expansively. 'Ah, new acquisitions,' she drawled. 'I am Eve-Ninedenine, Chief of Cyborg Operations. You're a protocol droid, aren't you?'

· 'I am See-Threepio.'

'Yes or no will do,' Ninedenine said icily.

'Well, yes,' Threepio replied.

'How many languages do you speak?' Ninedenine asked.

'I am fluent in over six million forms of communication and can ...'

'Splendid,' Ninedenine interrupted gleefully. 'We have been without an interpreter since the master got angry with something the last droid said, and disintegrated him.'

'Disintegrated!' Threepio wailed fearfully.

Ninedenine called a pig guard. 'This one will be quite useful. Fit him with a restraining bolt, then take him back to the main audience chamber.'

The guard shoved Threepio roughly towards the door. Artoo called out, but the guard grabbed him and pushed him out of the way.

Ninedenine laughed. 'I have need of you on the master's barge. Several of our droids have disappeared recently – stolen for spare parts, most likely.'

The droid on the torture rack emitted a high frequency wail, sparked briefly and was silent.

The court of Jabba the Hutt revelled in sordid ecstasy. Oola, the beautiful creature chained to Jabba, danced in the centre of the floor, as the drunken monsters round her cheered and heckled. Threepio hovered warily near the back of the throne. Periodically he had to duck to avoid fruit hurled at him or to sidestep a rolling body.

17

Jabba leered through his pipe smoke and beckoned Oola to sit beside him. She stopped dancing and, with a fearful look in her eye, backed away, shaking her head.

Jabba became angry. He pointed again to a spot beside him on the dais.

Oola shook her head more violently, her face a mask of terror.

Jabba's stare became livid. He pushed a button to release the chain by which Oola was tethered. Before she could flee, a trap-door in the floor dropped open and she tumbled into the pit below. There was a moment of silence followed by a terrified shriek, then once more silence.

Jabba laughed until he slobbered. A dozen revellers hurried over to peer through the grate and witness the nubile dancer's cruel end.

Threepio sank even lower, and looked for support to the carbonite form of Han Solo, suspended above him.

Suddenly, an unnatural silence fell over the room. Threepio looked up to see Bib Fortuna making his way through the crowd, accompanied by two Gamorrean guards and followed by a fierce-looking cloaked and helmeted bounty hunter who led his captive prize on a leash – Chewbacca, the Wookiee.

Threepio gasped, stunned. Chewbacca, too! The future looked very bleak indeed.

Bib muttered in Jabba's ear, pointing to the bounty hunter and his captive. The bounty hunter was humanoid, small and mean, with a belt of cartridges slung across his jerkin and an eye-slit in his helmet-mask. He bowed low, then spoke in fluent Ubese. 'Greetings, Majestic One. I am Boushh.'

Jabba answered in the same tongue, though his Ubese was stilted and slow. 'At last somebody has brought me the mighty Chewbacca … ' He tried to continue then decided to continue in Huttese. 'Where's my talkdroid?' he boomed, beckoning Threepio to come closer. 'Welcome our mercenary friend and ask his price for the Wookiee.'

Threepio translated his words. Boushh listened carefully, at the same time studying the evil creatures around the room and looking for possible escape routes. He particularly noticed Boba Fett standing near the door. He was the steel masked mercenary who had caught Solo.

Boushh spoke in his native tongue. 'I will take fifty thousand, no less.'

Threepio quickly translated for Jabba who immediately became outraged, knocking the droid off the dais with a sweep of his massive tail.

Boushh shifted his weapon to a more usable position. Jabba raved on in Huttese. Threepio struggled back onto the throne and translated for Boushh what Jabba was saying. 'Twenty-five thousand is all he'll pay.'

As two jawas covered Boushh, Jabba motioned his pig guards to take Chewbacca. Jabba spoke again. 'Twenty-five thousand and your life,' Threepio translated.

The room was silent, tense, uncertain. Finally, Boushh spoke. 'Tell that swollen garbage bag he'll have to do better than that, or they'll be scraping his smelly hide out of every crack in this room. I'm holding a thermal detonator.' Partially concealed, he held a small silver ball in his left hand.

'Well, what did he say?' Jabba barked at the droid.

Threepio prepared himself for the worst, then said in fluent Huttese, 'Boushh respectfully disagrees with Your Exaltedness and begs you to reconsider the amount or he will release the thermal detonator he is

19

holding.'

Instantly everyone in the room backed away. Jabba stared at the ball in the bounty hunter's hand. It was now beginning to glow.

Jabba stared for several more seconds then slowly a satisfied grin crept over his vast ugly mouth. A laugh rose from the pit of his belly like gas from a mire. 'The bounty hunter is my kind of scum. Tell him thirty-five, no more ... and warn him not to push his luck.'

Greatly relieved, Threepio translated. All eyes were on the bounty hunter.

Boushh released a switch on the thermal detonator, and it went dead. He nodded.

The crowd cheered. Jabba relaxed. 'Come, my friend. Join our celebration. I may find other work for you.'

Chewbacca growled under his breath as the Gamorreans led him away. Then, near the door, he spotted a familiar face. Behind a half-mask of pit-boar teeth was a human in the uniform of a skiff guard – Lando Calrissian. Chewbacca gave no sign of recognition: nor did he resist the guards who led him from the room.

Lando had infiltrated this nest of maggots much earlier, to see if it was possible to free Solo from Jabba's imprisonment. He'd done this for several reasons. First, he knew it was his fault that Han was in this predicament. Second, he wanted to join forces with Han's buddies at the top of the Rebel Alliance. Third, Princess Leia had asked him to help, and, finally, Lando would have bet anything that Han could not possibly be rescued from this place, and Lando just couldn't resist a bet.

Blending in here with the rest of the pirates was no problem for Lando, so he spent his days watching and calculating, like now as Chewie was led away.

Pig guards led Chewbacca through the unlit dungeon corridor. A tentacle coiled out of one of the doors to touch him. The next door was open. Chewie was hurled into the cell and the door slammed behind him, locking him in darkness.

He raised his head and let out a long pitiful howl that carried through the entire mountain of iron and sand and up into the endless sky.

A dark figure moved silently among the shadows, pausing behind a statue here, a column there. He made his way stealthily round the edge of the room, once stepping over a snoring Yak Face. He never made a sound. This was Boushh, the bounty hunter.

He reached the curtained alcove beside which the slab that was Hans Solo hung suspended. Looking round furtively, he flipped a switch beside the carbonite coffin and the heavy stone slowly lowered to the ground.

Boushh studied the space pirate's frozen face. He touched Solo's cheek curiously, as though it was a precious stone. Then, for a few seconds, he examined the controls beside the slab and activated a series of switches. Finally, he slid the decarbonization lever into place.

The casing began to emit a high-pitched sound. Anxiously, Boushh peered round, making certain that no one heard. Slowly, the hard shell that covered Solo's face started to melt away. Soon the coating was gone from the entire front of Solo's body, freeing his upraised arms to fall slackly to his side. Boushh extracted the lifeless body from the casing and lowered it gently to the floor.

He leaned close to Solo's face, listening for signs of life. No breathing. No pulse. He waited. Han's eyes snapped open with a start, and he began to cough. Boushh steadied him and tried to keep him quiet, in case the guards heard.

Han squinted at the dim form above him. 'I can't see. What's happening?' Having been in suspended animation for six of this desert planet's months, he was, understandably, disorientated.

Where was he now? What had happened? His last image was of Boba Fett watching him turn into carbonite. Was this Fett again now, come to thaw him for more abuse? The air roared in his ears, his breathing was irregular, unnatural. He waved his hand in front of his face.

Boushh tried to reassure him. 'You're free of the carbonite, but you still have hibernation sickness. Your eyesight will return in time. Come, we must hurry to get out of this place.'

Han grabbed the bounty hunter, felt the grated face mask and drew back. 'I'm not going anywhere.' He began sweating profusely as his mind groped for answers. 'Who are you?' he demanded.

The bounty hunter reached up and pulled away his helmet, revealing underneath the beautiful face of Princess Leia. 'One who loves you,' she whispered, taking his face in her still gloved hands and kissing him tenderly on the lips.

CHAPTER TWO

Han strained to see her. 'Leia, where are we?'

'Jabba's palace. I've got to get you out of here ... quickly.'

He sat up shakily. 'Everything is a blur. I'm not going to be much help.'

She looked at her blinded love. She had travelled light years to find him, risking her life and losing hard-won time sorely needed by the Rebellion. Tears filled her eyes. 'We'll make it,' she promised him.

There was suddenly a repulsive swishing sound behind them. Han opened his eyes, but could still see nothing. Leia looked up to the alcove beyond and her gaze turned to one of horror. The curtain had been drawn away, and the entire area, floor to ceiling, was a gallery of the most disgusting denizens of Jabba's court — gawking, salivating, wheezing.

'What is it?' Han pressed.

An obscene cackle rose from the other side of the alcove. A Huttese cackle.

Han held his head. 'I know that laugh.'

The curtain on the far side now opened. There sat Jabba himself, Ishi Tib, Bib, Boba, and several guards, all cackling evilly. 'My, what a touching sight,' Jabba purred. 'Han, my boy, your taste in companions has improved, even if your luck has not.'

Even blind, Solo could slide into smooth talk. 'Listen, Jabba, I was on my way back to pay you when I got sidetracked. I'm sure that we can work this out.'

Jabba chuckled again. 'It's too late for that, Solo. You may have been the best smuggler once, but now you're Bantha fodder.' He gestured to his guards. 'Take him!'

Guards grabbed Leia and Han. They dragged the Corellian pirate away, while Leia continued to struggle where she stood. 'I will decide how to kill him later,' Jabba muttered.

Lando quickly moved forward from the rank of guards, took hold of Leia, and tried to lead her away.

Jabba stopped him. 'Wait! Bring her to me.'

Lando and Leia halted in mid-stride. Lando looked tense and uncertain. 'I'll be all right,' Leia whispered.

Threepio, who had been watching from behind Jabba, turned away in dread.

Leia stood tall before the loathsome monarch. Her anger ran high. 'We have powerful friends, Jabba. You will soon regret this.'

'I'm sure,' Jabba agreed sarcastically, 'but in the meantime, I will thoroughly enjoy the pleasure of your company.' He pulled her to himself until their faces were only inches apart. He pressed her body to his oily snake-like skin. She felt like killing him, but she kept her ire in check. The rest of these vermin could kill her before she could escape.

Threepio peeped out then immediately withdrew again. 'Oh no, I can't watch.' The foul beast Jabba poked his fat dripping tongue out and slobbered a beastly kiss squarely on the Princess's lips.

Han was thrown roughly into a dungeon; the door crashed shut behind him. He fell to the floor in the darkness then picked himself up and sat against the wall, trying to organize his thoughts.

Leia! His heart sank at the thought of what must be happening to her now. If only he knew where he was. He knocked on the wall behind him. Solid rock.

What could he do? Things were so bad it seemed that they could get no worse.

He heard a low, formidable snarl from the far corner of the cell, the growl of a large and angry beast. Quickly, he rose, his back against the wall. The creature bellowed and raced straight at him, grabbing him ferociously round the chest and lifting him several feet in the air.

Han was totally motionless. 'Chewie, is that you?'

The giant Wookiee barked with joy and put him down, almost beside himself. Han reached up and scratched his partner's chest. Chewie cooed like a pup.

'What's going on round here?' Han was instantly down to business. Here was somebody he could make a plan with, his most loyal friend in the galaxy.

Chewie filled him in at length in a series of barks which few could understand.

'Lando's plan?' Han echoed. 'What's he doing here?'

Chewi barked more.

Han shook his head. 'Is Luke crazy? That kid can't take care of himself, let alone rescue anyone.'

Chewie disagreed and told him so.

'A Jedi Knight? Come off it. I'm out of action for a little while and everybody gets delusions.'

Chewi growled insistently.

Han nodded dubiously. 'I'll believe it when I see it,' he commented, walking straight into the wall. 'If you'll excuse the expression.'

*

The iron gate of Jabba's palace scraped open harshly. Standing outside in the dusty gale was Luke Skywalker. He was clad in the robe of a Jedi Knight, but wore neither gun nor lightsaber. He stood loosely, without bravado, taking measure of the place before entering. He was a man now, and wiser.

Finally, he strode into the arched hallway. Almost immediately two Gamorreans stepped up, blocking his path. Luke raised his hand and pointed at them. Before they could draw their weapons, they were clutching their own throats, choking, gasping. They fell to their knees.

Luke lowered his hand and walked on. The guards, now able to breathe again, did not follow him.

Around the corner, Luke was met by Bib Fortuna. Fortuna began speaking as he approached the young Jedi, but Luke didn't break stride. Bib had to trot beside him. 'You must be the one called Skywalker. His Excellency will not see you.'

'I will speak to Jabba now,' Luke said evenly, never slowing his pace. At the crossing, several more guards fell in behind them.

Luke stopped suddenly and stared at Bib. He locked eyes with him and raised his hand slightly. 'You will take me to Jabba now.'

Bib looked stunned. What were his instructions? He suddenly remembered. 'I will take you to Jabba now,' he repeated.

He turned and walked down the twisting corridor that led to the throne chamber. Luke followed him into the gloom. 'You serve your master well,' he whispered in Bib's ear.

'I serve my master well,' Bib repeated dutifully.

As Luke and Bib entered Jabba's court, the level of tumult dropped as if Luke's presence had a cooling effect. The lieutenant and the Jedi Knight approached the throne. Luke saw Leia seated there by Jabba's belly, chained at the neck and dressed in the skimpy costume of a dancing girl. He sensed her pain but he dismissed it from his mind. He needed to focus his attention entirely upon Jabba.

Threepio peeped from behind the throne. 'At last, Master Luke has come to take me away from all this,' he beamed.

Bib stood before Jabba. 'Master, I present Luke Skywalker, Jedi Knight,' he said proudly.

'I told you not to let him in,' the slug growled in Huttese.

'I must be allowed to speak,' Luke said quietly.

'He must be allowed to speak,' Bib agreed.

Furious, Jabba slashed Bib across the face and sent him reeling to the floor. 'You weak-minded fool,' he roared. 'He's using an old Jedi mind trick.'

Luke let Jabba fill his mind completely. 'You will bring Captain Solo and the Wookiee to me.'

Jabba smiled grimly. 'Your mind powers will not work with me, boy. I was killing your kind when being a Jedi meant something.'

Luke's expression did not change. 'Nevertheless, I am taking Captain Solo and his friends. You can either profit from this or be destroyed. It's your choice but I warn you not to underestimate my powers.'

Jabba laughed like a lion threatened by a mouse.

Threepio, who had been listening, leaned forward to whisper to Luke. 'Master, you're standing ... ' A guard stepped forward and pushed him away.

Jabba cut short his laugh. 'There will be no bargaining, young Jedi. I shall enjoy watching you die.'

Luke raised his hand. A pistol jumped from a nearby guard's holster and landed in his palm. Luke pointed the weapon at Jabba.

'Boscka,' Jabba spat.

The floor below Luke suddenly dropped away, sending Luke and his guard crashing into the pit below. The trap-door immediately closed again. The beasts of the court rushed to peer through the grating.

'Luke!' Leia cried. She started forward but was held by the manacle round her throat. A human guard touched her shoulder. It was Lando. Imperceptibly, he shook his head. This wasn't the right moment.

In the pit, Luke picked himself up from the floor. He was in a large, cave-like dungeon. The half-chewed bones of countless animals were strewn over the floor, smelling of decayed flesh and twisted fear. Twenty-five feet above him, he saw Jabba's repugnant courtiers peering at him through the grating.

The guard beside him suddenly began to scream as a door in the side of the dungeon started to open. Luke backed quickly to the wall and crouched, watching.

Out of the passage emerged the giant Rancor. The size of an elephant, it was somehow reptillian yet as unformed as a nightmare. Its huge screeching mouth was in the middle of its head: its fangs and claws out of proportion.

The guard picked up the pistol from the dirt where it had fallen and began firing laser bursts at the monster. This only made the beast angrier and it continued to advance.

The guard kept firing. Ignoring the blasts, the creature grabbed him, popped him into its slavering jaws and swallowed him. Then it started for Luke.

The Jedi Knight leaped twenty-five feet into the air and grabbed at the grating. Hand over hand, he crossed the grating to the corner of the dungeon, struggling to maintain his grip. One hand slipped and he

28

dangled precariously over the beast.

Two jawas ran to the top of the grate. They mashed Luke's fingers with their rifles. The watching crowd roared approval.

The Rancor pawed at Luke from below, but the young Jedi was just out of reach. Suddenly Luke released his hold and dropped, straight onto the howling monster's eye, then tumbled to the floor.

The beast screamed in agony. It ran in circles, then spotted Luke again and charged at him. Luke picked up a long bone of an earlier victim and brandished it before him. The monster grabbed Luke and drew him up to its salivating mouth. At the last moment, Luke wedged the bone deep into its throat and, as it began to gag, Luke jumped to the floor.

The Rancor, bellowing and flailing, ran headlong into a wall. Several rocks were dislodged, starting an avalanche which nearly buried Luke as he crouched in a crevice. The watching crowd continued to cheer.

Quickly, the choking beast dislodged the bone from its throat and, enraged, scrabbled through the rubble in search of Luke. Luke, peering round the pile, saw past the monster to a holding cave beyond, and beyond that again, a door.

The monster spotted Luke and made to grab him again. Luke grabbed a large rock and smashed it down on the monster's fingers. As it jumped, howling in agony, he ran for the holding cave.

He reached the door. Now a heavy barred gate blocked his way. Outside, the Rancor's two keepers were eating dinner. They looked up as they saw Luke and came towards the gate,

Luke turned to see the enraged monster coming after him. The keepers poked at him through the bars with their two-pronged spears, laughing as the Rancor drew close. Luke backed against the side wall. Suddenly he saw the restraining door control panel half way up the opposite wall. He seized a skull from the floor and threw it.

The panel exploded in a shower of sparks and the giant overhead iron gate came crashing down onto the Rancor's skull, crushing it like an over ripe melon.

The court above gasped. Jabba was apoplectic with rage. Leia was unable to hide her smile. This made Jabba even angrier. 'Get him out of there,' he snapped at his guards. 'Fetch me Solo and the Wookiee too. They will all suffer for this outrage.'

In the pit below, Luke waited calmly as Jabba's henchmen ran in to clap him in bonds and usher him out.

Han and Chewie were led before Jabba. Han still squinted and stumbled every few feet. Threepio hovered fearfully behind the Hutt. Jabba had Leia on a short tether, stroking her hair in an effort to calm himself. The rabble wondered what was going to happen next.

Several guards, including Lando Calrissian, dragged Luke into the room. The courtiers parted to give them passage. Before the throne, Luke nudged Solo. 'Good to see you, old buddy.'

Solo's face lit up. 'Luke, are you in this mess now, too? How are we doing?' Suddenly a bleak thought chilled him. 'Where's Leia? Is she ...'

Leia's eyes had been fixed on him from the moment he'd been dragged into the room. She called from Jabba's throne, 'I'm fine but I don't know how long I can hold off your slobbering friend here.' She spoke lightly to put Solo at ease. Han, Luke, Chewie, Lando — even Threepio: the sight of all her friends here at once made her feel nearly invincible.

Suddenly Jabba roared for Threepio. Timidly, the droid stepped forward and addressed the captives. 'His High Exaltedness has decreed that you are to be terminated immediately.'

'That's good. I hate long waits,' Solo said defiantly.

'Your extreme offence against His Majesty,' Threepio went on, 'demands the most torturous form of death. You will be taken to the Dune Sea, where you will be thrown into the Great Pit of Carkoon ...'

'That doesn't sound too bad,' Solo muttered to Luke.

' ... the resting place of the all-powerful Sarlacc. In his belly you will find a new dimension of pain and suffering as you slowly digest for a thousand years.'

Luke smiled. 'You should have bargained, Jabba. This is the last mistake you will ever make.'

Jabba chortled evilly. 'Take them away,' he ordered.

A loud cheer rose from the crowd. Leia caught a glimpse of Luke's face as the prisoners were dragged away. She was heartened to see that he was smiling.

Jabba's giant anti-gravity Sail Barge glided slowly over the endless Dune Sea. Its sand-blasted iron hull creaked in the breeze, each puff of wind coughing into the two huge sails. Jabba was below deck with most of his court.

Alongside the barge, two small skiffs floated in formation, one an escort craft carrying six scruffy soldiers: the other a gun skiff, carrying the three prisoners. They were all in bonds, and surrounded by guards – Barada, Weequays ... and Lando Calrissian. Lando kept quiet, waiting for his opportunity.

Han's eyes were still useless, but he kept his ears tuned. He spoke with reckless disregard to the guards to put them at ease, so that when the time came for him to make his move, they would be caught off balance. 'I think my sight is getting better,' he said, squinting over the sand.

'Believe me, you're not missing much,' Luke retorted. 'I grew up here.'

Luke thought of his youth on Tatooine, living on his uncle's farm, cruising the monotonous dunes in his souped-up landspeeder, and trying to avoid the peevish Tusken Raiders who guarded the sand as if it was gold dust.

He had met Obi-Wan Kenobi here – old Ben Kenobi, the hermit who had lived in the wilderness for longer than anyone remembered. This was the man who had first shown Luke the way of the Jedi.

Ben had taken Luke to Mos Eisley, the pirate city on the western face of Tatooine, where they'd first met Han Solo, and Chewbacca, the Wookiee. That was after Imperial stormtroopers had murdered Uncle Owen and Aunt Beru, as they searched for the fugitive droids, Artoo and Threepio.

That was how it all started for Luke. 'I grew up here,' he repeated softly.

'And now you're going to die here,' Solo retorted. 'If this is your big plan, I'm not crazy about it.'

'Jabba's palace was too well guarded,' Luke replied. 'I had to get you out of there. Just stay close to Chewie and Lando. We'll take care of everything.'

Jabba sat in the main cabin of the Sail Barge, surrounded by his retinue. Threepio was out of his depth. At the moment, he was being made to translate an argument between Ephant Mon, a bulky upright creature with an ugly tusked snout, and Ree-Yees. On Ephant Mon's shoulder sat Salacious Crumb, who repeated everything that Ephant said.

Threepio didn't really want to translate Ephant's words to Ree-Yees. The three-eyed goat-face was already drunk. But he did. Immediately, Ree-Kees's eyes dilated in fury. He punched Ephant Mon on the snout, sending him flying into a school of Squid Heads.

See-Threepio took this opportunity to slip to the rear, where he promptly bumped into a small droid, serving drinks. The stubby droid let out an irate series of beeps, toots and whistles. Threepio looked down in utter relief. 'Artoo, what are you doing here? This place is dangerous. They're going to execute Master Luke and, if we're not careful, us too!'

Jabba chuckled to see Ephant Mon go down. His swollen fingers tugged on the chain attached to Princess Leia's neck and drew her close to him. 'Don't stray too far, my lovely. Soon you will begin to appreciate me.' He pulled her even closer and, to her disgust, forced her to drink from his glass.

The convoy was stopping over a huge sand pit. The Sail Barge moved to one side with the escort skiff. The prisoners' skiff hovered directly over the pit, twenty feet in the air.

At the bottom of the deep cone of sand, a repulsive, mucous-lined, pink membranous hole puckered, almost unmoving. The hole was eight feet in diameter, and lined with three rows of inward-facing needle-sharp teeth. This was the mouth of the Sarlacc.

An iron plank was extended over the side of the prisoners' skiff. Two guards untied Luke's bonds and shoved him onto the plank, straight above the mouth in the sand, which was now beginning to salivate as it smelled meat.

Jabba moved his party onto the observation deck.

Luke rubbed his wrists to restore circulation. He

saw Leia standing at the rail of the big barge, and winked. She winked back.

Jabba motioned Threepio to his side and mumbled his orders. The golden droid stepped up to the comlink. 'His Excellency hopes that you will die honourably,' he announced, 'but if any of you wish to beg for mercy, Jabba will not listen to your pleas.'

Han stepped forward. 'Tell that slimy piece of worm-ridden filth ...'

Unfortunately, he was facing the desert, away from the Sail Barge. Chewie turned him round. Han continued without stopping, ' ... worm-ridden filth that he'll get no such pleasure from us.'

Luke was ready. 'Jabba, this is your last chance,' he called. 'Free us or die.' He shot a quick glance at Lando, who had moved to the back of the skiff.

Jabba raised his hand. 'I'm sure you're right, my young Jedi friend,' he sneered. Then he turned down his thumb. 'Put him in.'

Luke was prodded to the end of the plank. He looked up to see Artoo, standing alone by the rail, and flipped the little droid a jaunty salute. At this pre-arranged signal, a flap opened in Artoo's domed head, and a projectile shot straight into the air.

Luke jumped off the plank, but not to his doom. In a flash, he spun around in free fall, and caught the end of the plank with his fingertips. The thin metal bent wildly under his weight, then catapulted him up. He turned in mid-air and landed on the plank again, now facing the skiff. Casually, he extended his hand, and the lightsaber which Artoo had shot towards him landed neatly in his palm.

With Jedi speed, Luke ignited his sword and attacked the guard at the skiff edge, sending him screaming overboard into Sarlacc's twitching mouth.

34

The other guards swarmed towards Luke. Grimly, he waded into them, lightsaber flashing.

This was his own lightsaber, not his father's. He had lost his father's in the duel with Darth Vader which cost him his hand ... Darth Vader, who had told Luke that he was his father. This lightsaber Luke had fashioned himself in Obi-Wan Kenobi's abandoned hut on Tatooine, using the old Master Jedi's tools and parts. He wielded it now as if it were an extension of his arm, cutting through the onslaught like a light dissolving shadows.

Lando grappled with the helmsman, trying to seize control of the skiff. The helmsman's laser pistol fired, blasting the nearby panel. The skiff lurched to one side, throwing another guard into the Sarlacc's waiting jaws, and knocking the rest into a pile on the deck.

Luke picked himself up and ran towards the helmsman, lightsabre raised. He retreated, stumbled, then he, too, went over the side and into the pit.

When Jabba saw what was happening, he exploded with rage and yelled furious commands at everyone around him. Immediately, there was uproar, with creatures running in every direction.

It was during this confusion that Leia acted. She jumped onto Jabba's throne, grabbed the chain which enslaved her and wrapped it round his throat. Then she dived off, pulling the chain violently. The metal links buried themselves in the loose folds of the Hutt's neck, like a garotte.

With superhuman strength, she continued to pull. Jabba bucked his huge torso, nearly breaking her fingers and yanking her arms from their sockets. But Leia's hold was not merely physical. The Force was with her.

Jabba thrashed wildly as the chain dug deeper into

35

his neck, frantically trying to escape from this least expected foe. With a last gasping effort, he tensed every muscle and lurched forward. His reptilian eyes bulged from their sockets; his oily tongue flopped from his mouth. His thick tail twitched in spasms of effort ... then, finally, he lay still.

As Leia set about freeing herself, the battle outside began to rage. Boba Fett lit his rocket pack, leaped into the air and flew down from the barge to the skiff, just as Luke freed Han and Chewie from their bonds. Boba aimed his laser gun but before he could fire, the young Jedi swung round and sliced the bounty hunter's gun in half with his lightsaber.

A series of blasts from the large cannon on the barge hit the skiff broadside and set it rocking. Lando was tossed from the deck. At the last moment, he grabbed a strut and dangled precariously above the Sarlacc.

The skiff took another direct hit, throwing Han and Chewie against the rail. Wounded, the Wookiee howled in pain. Luke looked over at him and in that moment of distraction, Boba Fett fired out a cable from his armoured sleeve.

The cable wrapped around Luke several times, pinning his arms to his side and leaving his sword arm free from only the wrist down. He bent his wrist so that the lightsaber pointed upwards, then he spun towards Boba. The lightsaber cut through the cable instantly and Luke shrugged it away, just as another blast from the barge knocked Boba unconscious.

This explosion also dislodged the strut from which Lando was dangling, sending him careering into the Sarlacc pit. He hit the sandy slope, shrieked for help and tried to scramble out. But the loose sand tumbled him deeper into the gaping hole.

'Don't move!' Luke screamed, but his attention was

diverted by an incoming second skiff, full of guards firing weapons. Luke leaped directly into the centre of the skiff and immediately began annihilating them with lightning sweeps of his lightsaber.

Back in the other skiff, Chewie untangled himself from the wreckage, as Han struggled blindly to his feet. Chewie barked, trying to direct him to a spear lying on the deck.

Lando screamed, sliding closer to the Sarlacc's glistening jaws.

'Don't move, Lando,' Hans called. 'I'm coming.' His groping hand locked onto the spear.

Boba Fett rose, still a little dizzy. He looked over to the other skiff and saw Luke locked in battle with six guards. He steadied himself with one hand against the rail and aimed his weapon at Luke with the other.

'Which way?' shouted Han.

Chewie barked a reply. The space pirate swung the spear in Boba's direction. Fett blocked the blow with his forearm and again aimed at Luke. 'Get out of my way, you blind fool,' he cursed Han Solo.

Han swung his spear again, landing a hit square in the middle of Boba's rocket pack. The impact ignited the rocket. Boba blasted off, shooting over the second skiff like a missile, and ricocheting straight into the pit. His armoured body slid past Lando, straight into the Sarlacc's hungry mouth.

Chewie told Han what had happened. 'I wish I could have seen that,' Han chuckled.

Another hit from the barge's deck gun flipped the skiff onto its side, sending Han and almost everything else overboard. Han's foot caught in the railing, leaving him swinging dangerously above the Sarlacc. The wounded Wookiee clung tenaciously to the twisted debris astern.

Luke finished with his adversaries on the skiff, and leaped across the chasm of sand to the huge barge. Slowly, he began a hand to hand climb towards the deck gun.

Meanwhile, on the observation deck, Leia continued to struggle with the chain that bound her. Eventually Artoo came to her rescue. He zipped up to her, extended a cutting appendage from the side of his casing and cut through her bonds. 'Good work, Artoo,' she said. 'Now let's get out of here.'

They raced to the door. Threepio was lying on the floor screaming as a giant tuberous hulk named Hermi Odle sat on him. Salacious Crumb crouched by the droid's head, picking at his right eye.

Artoo sent a bolt of charge into Hermi Odle's backside, sending him wailing through a window. A similar flash blasted Salacious to the ceiling. Threepio quickly rose, his eye dangling from a sheaf of wires, and the two droids followed the Princess through the back door.

Holding on desperately with his injured arm, Chewie was stretched over the rail, grasping the dangling Solo's ankle. In turn, Solo was sightlessly reaching down for the terrified Calrissian. Lando had managed to stop his slide by lying very still, but every time he reached for Solo's outstretched hand, the loose sand edged him nearer to the hungry hole.

The deck gunners on the barge were lining up this living chain in their sights. Luke stepped in front of them, laughing like a pirate king. He lit his lightsabre before they could press the trigger: a moment later, they were smoking corpses.

A company of guards rushed up the steps from the lower decks, firing. One of the blasts shot Luke's lightsaber from his hand. He ran down the deck but was quickly surrounded. Two of the guards manned the deck gun again. Luke looked at his hand: the complex steel and circuit construction that replaced his real hand, which Vader had cut off in their last encounter.

The deck gunners re-opened fire on the skiff. The shock wave nearly knocked Chewie loose but, in tipping the skiff farther, Han was able to grab Lando's wrist. 'Pull,' he yelled at the Wookiee.

Calrissian screamed. One of Sarlacc's tentacles had wrapped itself round his ankle.

The deck gunners realigned their sights for the final kill, but it was all over for them before they could fire. Leia had commandeered the second deck gun at the other end of the barge. Her first shot blasted away the rigging and the second disposed of the gun crew.

The explosions on the barge momentarily distracted the five guards surrounding Luke. He reached out his hand and the lightsaber, lying on the deck ten feet away, flew to it. He leaped into the air as two of the guards fired at him and their laser bolts killed each other. Landing, he swung his blade and mortally wounded the others.

Meanwhile, the tug-of-war between Solo and Sarlacc, with Lando Calrissian as the rope, was continuing. Chewie braced himself against the rail and, holding Han's leg with one hand, he succeeded in pulling a laser gun from the wreckage with the other. He aimed the gun towards Lando, then lowered it, barking his concern.

Solo looked up. 'Chewie, pass the gun to me,' he cried. He took it with one hand, still holding Lando with the other.

'Hey, I thought you were blind,' Lando protested.

'I'm better. Trust me,' Han assured him. He

squinted, pulled the trigger and scored a direct hit on the tentacle. The wormy arm released its grip, slithering back into Sarlacc's mouth.

Chewbacca pulled mightily, drawing first Solo back into the boat, then Lando.

Luke, meantime, gathered Leia up in his left arm, while with his other he grabbed a rope from the rigging. He kicked the trigger of the second deck gun with his foot. As the gun exploded, he jumped into the air.

The two of them swung on the swaying rope down to the empty escort skiff. Luke steered it across to the floundering prison skiff and helped Chewbacca, Han and Lando on board.

The Sail Barge continued to explode behind them. Half of it was now on fire. Luke guided the skiff to the side of the barge where Threepio's legs were sticking straight up from the sand. Beside them, only Artoo's periscope was visible.

The skiff stopped just above them. Luke lowered a large electro-magnet from the helm. With a loud clang, the two droids shot out of the sand, locked to the magnet's plate. Now they were all in the skiff together.

There was a long moment of hugging, laughing, crying, beeping. Then somebody accidentally squeezed Chewbacca's wounded arm. His bellow reminded them that they still had much to do.

As the little skiff flew quietly off across the desert, the great Sail Barge settled slowly in a chain of explosions and violent fires. Finally it disappeared in a brilliant conflagration that was only partially diminished by the scorching afternoon light of Tatooine's twin suns.

CHAPTER THREE

The seven heroes walked step by step through the sandstorm, holding onto each other so as not to get lost. Artoo was first, following the signal of the homing device that was calling them. Threepio came next, then Leia, who was guiding Han, and finally Luke and Lando, supporting the hobbling Wookiee.

Artoo bleeped and they all looked up. Vague dark shapes could be seen through the typhoon.

For a few steps, the dark shapes grew darker: then, out of the darkness, the *Millennium Falcon* appeared, flanked by Luke's X-wing and a two-seater Y-wing. As soon as the group huddled beneath the *Falcon*'s bulk, the wind dropped a little. Threepio hit a switch, and the gangplank lowered with a hum.

Luke started towards his X-wing. Han stopped him. 'Thanks for coming after me, Luke,' he said quietly.

'Forget it,' Luke replied. He saw that a change had come over his friend. It was a gentle moment that he would treasure.

Chewie growled affectionately at the young Jedi warrior, mussing his hair like a proud uncle. Leia warmly hugged him. 'I'll see you back at the Fleet,' Luke promised.

'Why don't you come with us instead?' Han suggested.

'I have a promise to keep ... to an old friend,' Luke replied. He made for his X-wing and Artoo followed.

The others watched for a moment, trying to see their futures in the swirling sand. Lando jarred them into action. 'Come on. Let's get off this miserable dirt ball.'

Solo clapped him on the back. 'I guess I owe you some thanks too, Lando.'

Lando laughed. 'I figured that if I left you frozen like that, you'd bring me bad luck all my life.'

'He means "you're welcome",' smiled Leia.

They all headed up the ramp into the *Falcon*. Solo gave his ship a little pat. He was the last to enter.

In the X-wing Luke started up the engines and felt the comfortable roar. For the second time in his life, he rocketed off his home planet into the stars.

The Super Star Destroyer rested in space above the half-completed Death Star battle station and its green neighbour, Endor. The Destroyer was a massive ship, flanked by numerous smaller warships of various kinds which hovered and darted around their mother ship in endless activity.

The main bay of the Destroyer opened silently. An Imperial shuttle emerged and accelerated towards the Death Star, escorted by four squadrons of fighters.

Darth Vader watched their approach on the view-screen in the Death Star's control room. When they came close to docking, he marched out of the control room, followed by Commander Jerjerrod and a phalanx of Imperial stormtroopers, and headed towards the docking bay. He was about to welcome his master.

When he entered the docking bay, thousands of Imperial troopers snapped to attention. The shuttle came to rest on the pod. Its ramp lowered like a dragon jaw, and the Emperor's Royal Guard ran down, their red robes flapping. They formed a row on either side of the ramp. Silence filled the great hall. At the top of the ramp, the Emperor appeared.

Commander Jerjerrod and Darth Vader kneeled before him. He motioned them to rise and nodded for Vader to follow him to talk in private.

'The Death Star will be completed on schedule, my Master,' Vader assured him.

'Good,' said the Emperor. 'You have done well. Now I sense that you wish to continue your search for Luke Skywalker?'

Vader's breathing quickened beneath his mask. The wily Emperor always knew what was in his heart. 'Yes, my Master.'

'My friend, you must show patience,' the Emperor cautioned. 'In time, *he* will seek you. When he does, you must bring him before me. Only together can we turn him to the dark side.'

Vader bowed his head. Together, they would corrupt the boy. The Rebels of the galaxy would be shattered by the loss, and Vader would remain to rule, with the boy by his side. As it was always meant to be.

The Emperor raised his head, considering all possible futures. 'Everything is proceeding as I have foreseen.' He, like Vader, had his own plans. He savoured the nearness of his victory, the final seduction of the young Skywalker.

Luke left his X-wing parked on the edge of the water and picked his way through the adjoining swamp. Heavy mists swirled in layers about him.

He had terribly mixed feelings about this place. Dagobah ... where he had truly learned to be a Jedi and to use the Force, letting it flow through him to whatever end he directed it.

Dangerous creatures lurked in the swamp but to a Jedi, none was evil. Luke knew them all, for they were all part of the living planet and of the Force of which he, too, was an aspect. Yet there were dark things here too. He had seen them. Some he had run from and others he had vanquished.

The jungle thinned a bit. Beyond the next bog, Luke saw it — the small, strangely shaped dwelling, its odd little windows shedding a warm yellow light in the damp rain forest. He skirted the mire and, crouching low, he entered the cottage.

Yoda stood smiling, his small green hand clutching his walking stick for support. 'Waiting for you, I was,' he beamed. He motioned Luke to sit.

The boy was shocked by how much more frail Yoda had become. It was hard for him not to betray his concern at his old master's condition.

'That face you make,' Yoda chuckled. 'Look I so bad to young eyes?'

'No, Master ... of course not.'

'I do ... I do,' Yoda insisted cheerfully. 'Sick, I've become. Old and weak. When nine hundreds years you reach, look as good you will not.' He hobbled to his bed. 'Soon I will rest. Yes, forever sleep. Earned it, I have.'

Luke shook his head. 'You can't die, Master Yoda. I won't let you.'

'Trained well, and strong with the Force you are, but you are not that strong! This is the way of things ... the way of the Force.'

'But I need your help,' Luke protested. 'I want to complete my training.'

'No more training do you require,' Yoda assured him.

'Then I am a Jedi?' Luke pressed. In his heart, he knew that he was not.

Yoda's wizened features wrinkled. 'Not yet. One thing remains. Vader you must confront. Then, only then, a full Jedi you'll be. And confront him you will, sooner or later.'

Luke knew that Vader was at the core of his struggle. It was agonizing for him to put his vital question into words. 'Master Yoda ... is Darth Vader my father?'

Yoda's eyes filled with compassion. A sad smile creased his face. 'A rest, I need.'

Luke stared at the fading teacher, trying to give him strength with the force of his love and will. 'Yoda, I must know,' he whispered.

'Your father, he is,' Yoda said simply.

Luke closed his eyes, trying to shut his mind from the truth.

'Told you, did he?' Yoda asked.

Luke nodded, but did not speak.

'Unfortunate, this is,' said Yoda.

'Unfortunate that I know the truth?' Luke demanded bitterly.

Yoda raised himself with great effort. 'Unfortunate that you rushed to face him with your training incomplete ... that not ready for the burden, were you. Obi-Wan would have told you long ago, had I let him. Fear for you, I do.' He closed his eyes.

'Master Yoda, I am sorry,' Luke said.

'Sorry will not help.' Yoda beckoned Luke to his side. 'Remember, a Jedi's strength flows from the Force. Beware of anger, fear and aggression. The dark side are they. Easy they flow, quick to join you in a fight. Once you start down the dark path, forever it will dominate your destiny.'

He lay back, fighting for breath. Luke waited quietly, afraid of distracting the old Jedi. After a few minutes, he looked at the boy once more. 'Luke, of the Emperor, beware. Do not underestimate his power, or suffer your father's fate, you will. When I am gone, the last of the Jedi, you will be. Luke, the Force is strong in your family. Pass ... on ... what ... you ... have ... learned.' He began to falter and closed his eyes. 'There ... is ... another ... sky.'

Luke stared at his old Master's wasted body, wishing for the strength to bring him back to life. He felt a presence behind him. He turned. There was the image of Obi-Wan Kenobi. 'Ben,' he whispered hoarsely. There were so many things he wanted to say, but only one question sprang to his lips. 'Why, Ben?' he pleaded. 'Why didn't you tell me?'

'I was going to tell you when you finished your training,' the image of Ben replied. 'But you found it necessary to rush in, unprepared. I warned you about impatience.'

'You told me Darth Vader betrayed and murdered my father.' Luke was as bitter with Ben now as he had been with Yoda earlier.

Ben remained calm. 'Your father, Anakin, was seduced by the dark side of the Force. When that happened, the good man who was your father was destroyed.'

Luke did not speak.

'I don't blame you for being angry,' Ben coaxed. 'If I was wrong, it wasn't for the first time. You see, what happened to your father was my fault.'

Luke looked up with sudden interest. He'd never heard this before. He waited for Ben to continue.

'When I first met your father,' Ben went on, 'he was already a great pilot. The Force was strongly with him.

46

I took it upon myself to train him in the ways of the Jedi. My mistake was thinking that I could be as good a teacher as Yoda. I was not.

'The Emperor sensed Anakin's power, and he lured him to the dark side. My pride had terrible consequences for the galaxy.'

Luke was entranced. It was horrible that Obi-Wan could have caused his father's fall, but it was even more horrible that the dark side could strike so close to home, turning right to wrong. Yet Darth Vader must have a spark of Anakin Skywalker in him somewhere. 'There must still be good in him,' he declared.

Ben shook his head. 'I also thought that he could be turned back to the good side. It couldn't be done. He is more machine than man now – twisted and evil.'

Luke sensed what Kenobi was trying to tell him. He shook his head. 'I can't kill my own father.'

'You mustn't think of that machine as your father.' He spoke now as a teacher again. 'When I saw what had become of him, I tried to bring him back. We fought. Your father fell into a molten pit. When he clawed his way out, the change had been burned in him for ever. He was Darth Vader, without a trace of Anakin Skywalker. He is kept alive only by machinery and his own dark will.'

Luke looked down at his own mechanical right hand. 'I tried to stop him once. I couldn't do it.'

'Vader humbled you when first you met him, Luke, but that experience was part of your training. It taught you, among other things, the value of patience. Had you not been so impatient to defeat Vader then, you could have finished your training here with Yoda. You'd have been prepared.'

'But I had to help my friends,' Luke protested.

'Did you help them? It was left to them to save you.

47

You achieved nothing.'

'I found out that Darth Vader is my father,' Luke reminded him sadly.

'To be a Jedi, you must confront and go beyond the dark side. Impatience is the easiest door – for you, like your father. Only your father was seduced by what he found beyond the door, and you have held firm. You're no longer reckless, Luke. You are ready for your final confrontation.'

Luke shook his head again. 'I can't do it, Ben.'

Obi-Wan Kenobi's shoulders slumped in defeat. 'Then the Emperor has already won. You were our only hope.'

Luke reached for alternatives. 'Yoda said I could train another to …'

CHAPTER FOUR

Darth Vader stepped out of the long cylindrical elevator into the Emperor's throne room. Two Royal Guards stood either side of the door, red robes from neck to toe, red helmets covering all but eye-slits. Their weapons were always drawn.

Sitting in an elaborate control-chair, staring out of a huge, circular observation window, was the Emperor. Immediately beyond the window was the uncompleted half of the Death Star, shuttles and transports buzzing round it, and men with tight-suits and rocket-packs doing exterior construction on the surface. Farther out, the jade-green moon Endor rested like a jewel in space.

The Emperor drank in the view with a sense of glory. This was all his.

It hadn't always been so. Back in the days when he was merely Senator Palpatine, the galaxy had been a Republic of stars, cared for and protected by the Jedi Knighthood which had watched over it for centuries. But the Republic grew too large and corruption set in.

A few greedy senators set off a chain reaction ... and suddenly there was a fever in the stars. Fear had spread like an epidemic.

Senator Palpatine had seized the moment. Through fraud and false promises, he had himself elected head of the Council. Then, through assassination, subterfuge and terror, he named himself Emperor. The Republic had crumbled and the Empire was resplendent, because the Emperor knew what others refused to believe – the dark forces were the strongest. His soul was the black centre of the Empire.

Vader approached him from behind, kneeled and waited, but Vader did not mind. It was an honour to kneel at his ruler's feet.

Finally the chair slowly rotated until the Emperor faced Vader. Vader spoke first. 'What is thy bidding, my Master?'

'Send the fleet to the far side of Endor. There it will stay until called for.'

'But what of the reports of the Rebel fleet massing near Sullust?'

'That is of no consequence. Soon the Rebellion will be crushed and young Skywalker will be one of us. Your work here is finished, my friend. Go out to the command ship and await my orders.'

'Yes, my master.' Vader hoped that he would be given command over the destruction of the Rebel Alliance. He hoped that it would be soon.

In a remote vacuum beyond the edge of the galaxy, the vast Rebel fleet stretched beyond the range of human vision. Corellian battle ships, cruisers, destroyers, carriers, bombers, Sullustian freighters, Calamarian tankers, Alderaanian gunships, Kesselian blockade runners, X-wing, Y-wing and A-wing fighters, shuttles, transport vehicles, men o' war. Every Rebel in the galaxy, soldier and civilian alike, waited tensely in these ships for instructions. They were led by the largest of the Rebel Star Cruisers, the *Headquarters Frigate*.

Hundreds of Rebel commanders, of all species and

life forms, assembled in the war room of the giant star cruiser, awaiting orders from the High Command. At the centre of the briefing room was a large circular table, projected above which hovered images of the unfinished Imperial Death Star and the moon Endor, whose protective deflector encompassed them both.

Mon Mothma entered the room. A stately, beautiful woman of middle age, she wore white robes with gold braiding. She was the elected leader of the Rebel Alliance.

Like Leia's adopted father and like Palaptine the Emperor, Mon Mothma had been a senior senator of the Republic, a member of the High Council. Mon Mothma had remained a senator till the end, organising dissent and trying to stabilise the crumbling government.

Towards the end, she had organised pockets of resistance, each unaware of the identity of the rest. Each was responsible for inciting revolt against the Empire when it finally triumphed.

There had been other leaders, but many were killed when the Empire's first Death Star annihilated the planet Alderaan, where Leia's adopted father was killed. Mon Mothma went underground. She joined her followers with thousands of guerrillas and insurgents, spawned by the Empire's cruel dictatorship. Thousands more joined the Rebel Alliance. Mon Mothma became acknowledged leader of all the galaxy's creatures who had been left homeless by the Emperor.

She crossed the room to confer with her two chief advisers, General Madine and Admiral Ackbar. Madine was a Corellian, tough and resourceful. Ackbar was pure Calamarian, a gentle salmon-coloured creature with huge, sad eyes in a high-domed head, and webbed hands that made him more at home in water or free space than on board a ship. But, when pushed to the limit, Calamarians could fight with the best.

Lando Calrissian made his way through the crowd, scanning faces. He saw Wedge, who was to be his wing pilot. They nodded to each other, then Lando moved on. Finally, standing by a side door, he found who he was looking for.

Han, Chewie, Leia and the two droids greeted his appearance with a mixture of cheers, laughs, bleeps and barks. 'Well, look at you,' Han chuckled, pointing at Lando's insignia. 'A general, no less.'

Lando laughed. 'Somebody must have told them about my little manoeuvre at the battle of Tanaab.' Before his stint as Governor of Cloud City, Calrissian had wiped out the bandits on Tanaab against all odds, using legendary flying and unheard of strategies.

Han opened his eyes wide. 'Don't look at me. I merely told them that you're a fair pilot. I had no idea that they were looking for somebody to lead this crazy attack.'

'That's all right. I want to,' Lando assured him.

Han looked at his old friend with admiration and disbelief. 'Have you ever seen a Death Star? You'll be lucky if you're a general for very long, old buddy.'

'I'm surprised they didn't ask you to do it,' Lando smiled.

'Maybe they did,' Han retorted, 'but I'm not crazy.'

Leia moved closer to Han and took his arm. 'Han is going to stay on the command ship with me.'

Suddenly, in the middle of the room, Mon Mothma signalled for attention. The room fell silent. 'The date brought to me by the Bothan spies has been confirmed,' the leader announced. 'The Emperor has made a critical error, and the time for our attack has come. We now know the location of the Emperor's new battle station.

'The weapon systems on this Death Star are not yet operational. With the Imperial fleet spread throughout the galaxy in a vain effort to engage us, it is relatively unprotected.' She paused for a moment. 'More important, we have learned that the Emperor himself is personally overseeing the construction.'

A cheer rose from the assembly. This was what they had all been waiting for … a shot at the Emperor.

Mon Mothma waited for the hubbub to die down. 'His trip was taken in utmost security but he underestimated our spy network.' Her voice was suddenly stern. 'Many Bothans died to bring us this information.'

Admiral Ackbar stepped forward. He was an expert on Imperial defence procedures. He raised his fin and pointed to the model of the force field round Endor and the Death Star. 'Although uncompleted, the Death Star is not entirely without defence,' he said in soothing Calamarian tones. 'It is protected by an energy field which is generated on Endor. No ship can fly through it, nor any weapon penetrate it. The shield must be deactivated before any attack is attempted.' He pointed at the unfinished portion of the Death Star. 'Once the shield is down, the cruisers will create a perimeter, while the fighters fly into the superstructure and attempt to hit the main reactor — somewhere in here.'

Another murmur swept through the room.

'General Calrissian will lead the fighter attack,' Ackbar concluded.

He yielded the floor to General Madine. 'We have acquired a small Imperial shuttle,' Madine declared. 'Under this guise, a strike team will land on Endor and deactivate the shield generator. The control bunker is well guarded, but a small force should be able to penetrate their security.'

Leia turned to Han. 'I wonder who they've found to pull that one off?' she said, under her breath.

'General Solo, is your strike team assembled?' Madine called.

Leia, a little astonished, looked at Han admiringly. Since he emerged from Jabba's carbonization, a change had come over him. He wasn't a loner anymore. He had let himself become a member of the team.

'My squad is ready, Sir,' Solo responded, 'but I need a command crew for the shuttle.' He looked questioningly at Chewbacca.

Chewie nodded his head cheerfully, and raised a hairy paw.

'That's one,' Han called.

'Here's two,' Leia shouted, sticking her arm in the air.

'And I'm with you too,' called a voice from the back of the room.

Luke was standing at the top of the stairs. Cheers rose for the last of the Jedi.

Han was unable to conceal his joy.

Leia ran to Luke and hugged him warmly, but she quickly sensed a change in him. 'What is it, Luke?' she whispered.

'I'll tell you some day,' Luke murmured softly.

Han, Chewie, Lando and several others crowded round Luke with their greetings. Then the entire assembly dispersed. It was the time for last farewells.

The *Millenium Falcon* rested in the main dock bay of the Rebel Star Cruiser, being loaded and serviced. Just beyond it stood the stolen Imperial shuttle, looking out of place among the Rebel X-wing fighters.

Chewie supervised the final transfer of weapons and supplies to the shuttle.

Han stood with Lando between the two ships, saying goodbye — possibly for ever. Han nodded at *Falcon*. 'Go on. Take her,' he urged. 'You know she's the fastest ship in the whole fleet now.' The *Falcon* had always been fast, but after he won her from Lando, Han had souped her up, and now she was faster.

Lando knew this. 'Thanks, old buddy. I'll take good care of her.'

Solo looked warmly at the endearing rogue. 'You'd better,' he warned him.

Han entered the cockpit of the Imperial shuttle as Luke was doing some final tuning on a rear navigational panel. Chewbacca, in the co-pilot's seat, was trying to figure out the Imperial shuttles. Han took the pilot's seat and Chewie grumbled about the design.

'I don't think the Empire designed it with a Wookiee in mind,' Han grinned.

Leia entered from the hold and took a seat near Luke. 'We're all set back here,' she called.

'Rrrwfr,' said Chewie, hitting the first sequence of controls. He glanced at Han. The space pirate was looking wistfully back at the *Millenium Falcon*, thinking of the times he had saved her with his skill, and the times that she had saved him with her speed. He snapped back to the moment. 'Right, Chewie,' he said crisply. 'Let's see what this baby can do.'

They fired the stolen shuttle's engines, eased her out of the docking bay, and banked off into the endless night.

Construction on the Death Star continued. Traffic in

the area was thick with transport ships, TIE-fighters and equipment shuttles. Periodically the Super Star Destroyer orbited the area, surveying progress from every angle.

Suddenly, on the Destroyer's control deck, Controller Jhoff made contact with a shuttle of the Lambda class, approaching the shield from Sector Seven. 'Shuttle to Control, come in, please,' the voice called into Jhoff's headset.

'We have you on our screen now,' the controller replied into his comlink. 'Please identify.'

'This is shuttle *Tydirium* requesting deactivation of the deflector shield.'

'Transmit the clearance code for shield passage,' the controller ordered.

In the shuttle, Han threw a worried look at his companions and said into his comlink. 'Transmission commencing.'

Chewie flipped a bank of switches, producing a series of high-frequency transmissions.

Leia bit her lip. 'Now we'll find out if that code was worth the price we paid.'

Luke stared at the huge Super Star Destroyer that loomed in front of them. It filled his heart and mind with darkness. 'Vader is on that ship,' he muttered.

'You're just jittery, Luke,' Han assured him. 'There are lots of command ships.'

'They're taking a long time with that code clearance,' Leia said anxiously. What if they failed? The Alliance could do nothing if the Emperor's deflector shield remained functioning.

Han tried to cheer them up. 'Let's try to be optimistic,' he urged.

'He knows I'm here,' Luke avowed. The command ship seemed to be taunting him.

56

Lord Vader stood quite still, staring out of a large viewscreen at the Death Star. He thrilled to see this monument to the dark side of the Force.

Then, in the midst of his dreaming, he became absolutely motionless: not a breath, not a heartbeat stirred to mar his concentration. He strained his every sense. What had he felt?

He strode down the row of controllers to the tracking screen where Admiral Piett was standing over Controller Jhoff. 'Where is that shuttle going?' the Dark Lord demanded.

Piett spoke into his comlink. 'Shuttle *Tydirium*, what is your cargo and destination?'

'Parts and technical personnel for the Sanctuary Moon,' came the reply.

'Do they have clearance?' Vader questioned.

'It's an older code but it checks out,' Piett replied. He hoped that nothing was amiss. Lord Vader did not take mistakes lightly.

'I have a strange feeling about that ship,' Vader mused, almost to himself.

'Should I hold it?' Piett asked hastily, anxious to please his master.

'No, let it pass,' Vader ordered. 'I shall deal with this myself.'

In the shuttle *Tydirium*, the group waited tensely. The more questions they were asked, the more likely were they to break their cover. To their relief, the controller's voice came over the comlink. 'Shuttle *Tydirium*, deactivation of the shield will commence immediately. Follow your present course.'

Chewie barked loudly.

'What did I tell you?' Han grinned. He pushed the throttle forward, and the stolen shuttle moved smoothly towards the green Sanctuary Moon.

In the control room, Vader, Piett and Jhoff watched the viewscreen as the web-like deflector parted to admit the shuttle, which moved slowly towards the centre of the web – to Endor.

Vader turned to the deck officer. 'Ready my shuttle,' he ordered urgently. 'I must go to the Emperor.'

CHAPTER FIVE

The trees of Endor stood a thousand feet tall. Their trunks, covered with shaggy bark, rose straight as pillars. Their foliage was spindly, but lush in colour, scattering the sunlight in delicate blue-green patterns on the forest floor. The ground cover was mostly fern, so dense that it was like a green sea.

The stolen Imperial shuttle sat in a clearing many miles from the Imperial landing port, camouflaged with a blanket of dead branches and leaves. Its steely hull was dwarfed by the towering trees.

On a hill beside the clearing, the Rebel contingent was starting up a steep trail. Leia, Chewie, Han and Luke led the way, followed in single file by the ragged squad of the strike team. This unit was made up of the Rebel Alliance's toughest groundfighters, hand picked for their initiative, cunning and ferocity. And they all knew the importance of their mission. If they failed, the Rebellion was doomed.

Artoo-Detoo and See-Threepio brought up the rear of the party. Artoo's dome swivelled as he went, his sensor beams searching the trees that surrounded them.

Ahead, Chewie and Leia reached the crest of the hill. They dropped to the ground, crawled the last few yards and peered over the edge. Chewie raised his great paw, signalling the rest to stop. Suddenly, the forest seemed more silent.

Luke and Han edged forward on their bellies to view what Chewie and Leia had already seen. Not far below, in a glen beside a clear pool, two Imperial guards had set up a temporary camp. They were warming a meal over a portable cooker. Two rocket bikes were parked nearby.

'Should we try to go round them?' Leia whispered.

Luke shook his head. 'It will take too much time.'

'And if they catch sight of us and report, we're finished,' Han added.

Leia motioned the rest of the squad to stay, then she, Luke, Han and Chewbacca edged closer to the camp.

When they were close, Han slid into the lead position. 'Stay here,' he rasped. 'Chewie and I will take care of this.'

'Be careful,' Luke warned. 'There might be ...'

Before he could finish, Han and his furry partner jumped to their feet and rushed into the clearing. Leia and Luke flattened to the ground and watched.

Han was in a fist fight with one of the scouts. The other was already on his speeder bike, trying to escape. Before he could start the engine, Chewie fired a few shots from his crossbow-laser. The ill-fated guard crashed against an enormous tree.

Leia drew her laser pistol and raced into the battle, followed closely by Luke. As soon as they ran into the clearing, several large laser blasts went off all round them, throwing them to the ground. Leia lost her gun.

Dazed, they looked up to see two more Imperial scouts emerging from the forest, heading for their speeder bikes, hidden in the foliage. They holstered their pistols as they mounted their bikes, and fired the engines.

'I'll deal with this,' Luke said crisply, rising.

But Leia had her own ideas. She ran to the remaining speeder bike, fired it and took off in pursuit of the fleeing scouts. As she tore past Luke, he jumped onto the bike behind her. 'Quick, centre switch,' he shouted over her shoulder. 'Jam their comlinks.'

As Luke and Leia soared out of the clearing, Han and Chewie finished subduing their adversaries. 'Hey, wait!' he called, but Luke and Leia were out of sight.

The young Jedi and the Princess sped through the dense foliage, a few feet off the ground. The two escaping scouts had a good lead but, at two hundred miles an hour, Leia was the better pilot.

Occasionally she fired a burst from the speeder's laser cannon, but she was still too far behind to be accurate. 'Move closer!' Luke shouted.

Leia opened the throttle, closing the gap. The two scouts sensed their pursuer was closing on them and recklessly veered this way and that, skimming through a narrow opening between two trees. One of the speeders scraped the bark, nearly tipping the scout out of control and slowing him significantly.

'Get alongside,' Luke yelled.

She pulled her speeder close to the scouts and Luke suddenly leaped from Leia's bike onto his back. He grabbed him round the neck and flipped him off, then scooted forward to the driving seat. He grabbed the controls and set off after Leia who had pulled ahead.

The chase swung north and passed a gully where two more Imperial scouts were resting. Now they swung into pursuit, hot on Luke and Leia's tail, blasting with their laser cannons. Luke, still behind, took a glancing blow.

'Keep on that one,' Luke shouted, indicating the scout ahead. 'I'll take the two behind.'

Leia shot ahead. Luke flared his retro-rockets, slamming the speeder into rapid deceleration. The two scouts on his tail zipped past him, unable to slow down. Immediately, Luke switched to top speed again, firing with his blasters, suddenly in pursuit of his pursuers.

His third round hit its mark. One of the scouts, blown out of control, smashed against a boulder in a rumble of flame. His companion glanced at the flash and put his speeder in super-charge, moving even faster. Luke kept pace with him.

Ahead, Leia and the first scout continued their own high-speed chase through the massive trunks and low-slung branches. Suddenly Leia shot in the air and vanished from sight.

The scout turned in confusion, uncertain whether to relax or worry about his pursuer's sudden dis-appearance. Out of the treetops, Leia dived down on him, blasting from above.

Now her speed was even greater than she expected and in a moment, she was beside him. Seeing her, he reached for his handgun and fired.

Leia's speeder spun out of control. She jumped free just in time. As she rolled clear into a tangle of matted vines, the speeder exploded on a giant tree. The last thing she saw was an orange fireball. Then came blackness.

The scout looked back with a satisfied sneer but when he turned, he was on a collision course with a fallen tree. All was over but the flaming.

Meanwhile, Luke was closing on the last scout. As they weaved through the trees, Luke drew level with him. The scout swerved, slamming his speeder into Luke's. They both tipped precariously, barely missing a large fallen trunk. The scout zoomed under it and

Luke over it. When he came down on the other side, he crashed directly onto the other rider's vehicle. Their steering vanes locked.

The scout banked right, trying to smash Luke into an onrushing grove of saplings. Luke leaned all his weight left, turned the locked speeders horizontal, with him on top and the scout below.

The scout suddenly stopped resisting Luke's leftward leaning, and threw his weight in the same direction. As a result, the speeders flipped over in a full circle and came to rest upright again. Now an enormous tree loomed in front of Luke. Luke leaped from his speeder, which crashed into the redwood and exploded.

Luke rolled up a moss-covered slope. The scout swooped high, circling around and looking for him. Luke stumbled out of the bushes as the speeder bore down on him in full throttle, its laser cannon firing. Luke ignited his lightsaber and stood his ground.

The lightsaber deflected every bolt the scout fired, but the speeder kept coming, intent on slicing the young Jedi in half. Luke stepped aside with perfect timing, like a master bull fighter, and chopped off the speeder's steering vanes with a single mighty blow. The speeder shuddered, then pitched and rolled. In a second, it was out of control entirely to become a billow of fire in the forest.

Vader's shuttle swung around the unfinished portion of the Death Star and settled into the main docking bay. Silent bearings lowered the Dark Lord's ramp. His steps were soundless as he glided down the chilly steel.

The main corridor was filled with courtiers, all awaiting an audience with the Emperor. Pompous toadies with velvet robes and painted faces, perfumed bishops passing notes and judgments, oily favour merchants, bent low from the waist under the weight of stolen jewellery.

Vader had no patience with such petty filth. He passed them without a nod, though many of them would have paid dearly for a glance from him.

When he reached the elevator to the Emperor's tower, he found the door closed. Red-robed Royal Guards flanked the shaft, unaware of Vader's presence. An officer stepped from the shadows and confronted him. 'You may not enter,' he said evenly.

Vader wasted no words. He raised his fingers, outstretched, towards the officer's throat. The officer's knees started to buckle, his face turning grey as he gasped for air. 'It ... is ... the ... Emperor's ... command.'

'I will wait his convenience,' Vader said, releasing him. He turned to look out of the view window. Endor floated there, glowing in the black space like a torch in the night.

Han and Chewie crouched facing each other in the forest clearing. The rest of the Strike Force spread out around them in groups of two and three.

Even Threepio was silent. He sat beside Artoo, polishing his fingers for want of something to do. The others checked their watches or their weapons as the afternoon sunlight began to fade.

Suddenly Artoo bleeped.

Threepio ceased his polishing and peered apprehensively into the forest. 'Someone's coming,' he translated.

The rest of the squad faced out, weapons raised. A twig cracked beyond the western perimeter.

With a weary stride, Luke stepped out of the foliage.

**Darth Vader in the
Docking Bay of the new Death Star.**

C-3PO on the Sail Barge with members of Jabba's court.

Princess Leia enslaved by Jabba the Hutt

He flopped down on the hard earth beside Solo and lay back with an exhausted groan.

Solo looked into the forest from which Luke had emerged. 'Where's Leia?'

Luke looked up in alarm. 'She didn't come back?'

'I thought she was with you,' said Solo.

'We got split up,' Luke explained. 'We'd better go look for her.'

'Rest a while first,' Solo suggested.

'I want to find her,' Luke insisted.

Solo nodded. He signalled to the officer who was second in command of the strike team. 'Take the squad ahead,' he ordered. 'We'll rendezvous at the shield generator at 0-30.'

The officer saluted and immediately organized his troops. Within a minute they were filing silently into the forest, relieved to be on the move at last.

Luke, Chewbacca, Solo and the two droids set off in the opposite direction. Artoo led the way, his scanner sensing for his mistress.

The first thing Leia was aware of was her left elbow. It was lying in a pool of water and it was painful. Slowly, reluctant to see the extent of her wounds, she opened her eyes.

Things were blurred at first but they gradually came into focus ... and she saw the Ewok.

A little furry creature, he stood no more than three feet tall. He had large, curious, brownish eyes, stubby little finger paws, and was completely covered, head to foot, with brown fur. He looked like the baby Wookiee doll Leia played with as a child, except that he had a knife strapped to his waist and a thin leather mantle covering his head.

They looked at each other, unmoving. The Ewok

seemed puzzled by the Princess, uncertain of what she was or what she intended.

Leia sat up, with a groan. The sound frightened the Ewok. He rapidly stumbled backwards, tripped and fell. 'Eeeap!' he squeaked.

Leia examined herself carefully. Her clothes were torn and she had cuts and bruises all over her body, but nothing seemed to be broken. She groaned again, wishing that she knew where she was.

Frightened, the Ewok jumped up, grabbed a four-foot long spear, and pointed it defensively at her. Warily, he circled her, clearly more nervous than aggressive.

'Cut that out.' Leia brushed the weapon aside. More gently, she added, 'I'm not going to hurt you.'

Gingerly, she rose, testing her legs. The Ewok backed away cautiously. 'Don't be afraid,' Leia coaxed. 'I just want to see what's happened to my speeder.'

The Ewok followed her to the charred remains of the speeder, like a skittish puppy. Leia picked up the Imperial scout's laser pistol – all that was left of him.

Sitting down again, she buried her head in her hands. The Ewok sat down beside her and copied her posture exactly, even mimicking her sigh. Leia laughed and scratched his furry head.

Suddenly, he froze. His ears twitched: he sniffed the air.

'What is it?' Leia whispered. Then she heard it: a quiet snap, and rustling in the bushes. She drew her pistol.

The laser bolt came from where she least expected – high, off to the right. It exploded in front of the log with a shower of light. She returned the fire quickly – two short blasts, then she sensed something behind her.

66

Darth Vader in the
Docking Bay of the new Death Star.

C-3PO on the Sail Barge with members of Jabba's court.

Princess Leia enslaved by Jabba the Hutt

...ndo Calrissian struggling with one of the skiff guards

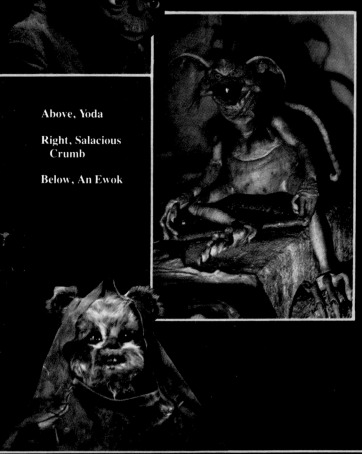

Above, Yoda

Right, Salacious
    Crumb

Below, An Ewok

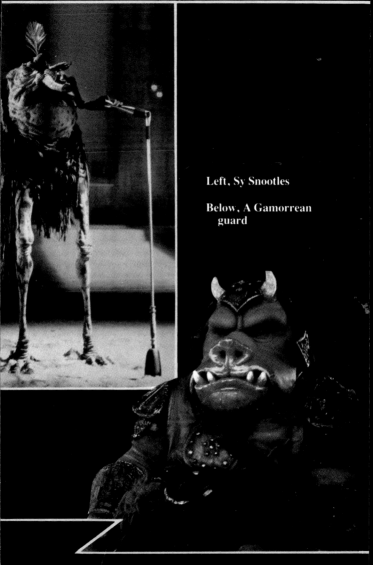

Left, Sy Snootles

Below, A Gamorrean
guard

Admiral Ackbar and one of the Mon Calamari.

Lando Calrissian, Chewbacca, and Han Solo in the Rebel
Briefing Room.

Luke and Leia in the Ewok village.

Han, Leia, and Chewie captured by Stormtroopers.

R2-D2 and Wicket

An Imperial scout was standing over her, his weapon levelled at her head. He reached out his hand for her pistol. 'I'll take that,' he snarled.

A scout officer emerged from the foliage.

Without warning, a furry hand came from under the log and jabbed the scout in the leg with a knife. The man howled with pain and danced from foot to foot.

Leia pounced on his laser pistol. She rolled, fired and hit him squarely in the chest, flash-burning his heart.

Now the forest was quiet again. Leia lay still, panting softly and waiting for another attack, but none came. The little Ewok, whose name she was to learn was Wicket, poked his furry head from under the log, and purred at her.

Leia rose to a crouch and looked all round. It seemed safe for the moment. She motioned to Wicket. 'Come on. Let's get out of here.'

As they moved into the thick flora, Wicket took the lead. Leia was unsure at first, but he shrieked urgently and tugged at her sleeve, so she followed him.

Lord Vader stepped out of the elevator and stood at the entrance to the throne room. He kneeled, motionless.

'Rise and speak, my friend,' the Emperor commanded.

'My master, a small Rebel force has penetrated the shield and landed on Endor,' Vader said.

'Yes, I know.' There was no hint of surprise in the Emperor's tone.

'My son is with them,' Vader went on.

The Emperor's brow furrowed slightly. 'Are you sure?'

'I felt him, my master.' It was almost a taunt. He knew that the Emperor, in his heart, was afraid of young Skywalker. Only together could Vader and he hope to pull the youthful Jedi Knight over to the dark side.

'Strange that I have not,' the Emperor murmured, his eyes becoming slits. He sensed something strange. Vader and his son were more closely linked than was the Emperor with young Skywalker. 'I wonder if your feelings on this matter are clear, Lord Vader?'

'They are clear, my master.' Vader could not mistake his son's presence.

'Then you must go to the Sanctuary Moon and wait for him,' the Emperor said simply.

'He will come to me?' Vader asked sceptically. He felt that the first move must come from him.

'Of his own free will,' the Emperor assured him. It had to be of Luke's own free will, else all was lost. A spirit could not be forced into corruption: it had to be tempted. 'I have foreseen it. His compassion for you will be his undoing.' Compassion had always been the Jedis' weakness. 'The boy will come to you and you will then bring him to me.'

Vader bowed low. 'As you wish, my master.' With that, he strode out of the throne room, to board the shuttle for Endor.

Luke, Chewie, Han and Threepio picked their way through the undergrowth behind Artoo, whose antennae revolved ceaselessly. It was remarkable how the little droid could blaze a trail over jungle terrain like this, the miniature cutting tools on his walkers and dome slicing neatly through anything too dense to be pushed out of the way.

Artoo suddenly stopped. His radar screen spun faster. He clicked and whirred to himself, then darted forward with an excited annoucement.

Threepio raced behind him. 'Artoo says the rocket speeders are right up ... oh dear.'

They broke into the clearing and spread out to inspect the rubble. The charred debris of three speeders was strewn around the area, and the remains of three scouts. But there was no evidence of Leia, except a torn piece of her jacket. Han examined it soberly.

'Artoo's sensors find no other trace of Princess Leia,' Threepio said quietly.

'I hope she's nowhere near here now,' Han muttered.

'It looks like she ran into two of them,' Luke said.

Only Chewbacca seemed uninterested in the clearing. He faced the dense foliage and wrinkled his nose, sniffing. 'Rahrr!' he roared, plunging into the thicket. The others rushed after him.

The trees became taller as the group pushed on, and the girth of their trunks increasingly massive. Then came another clearing. At its centre, a single tall stake was planted in the ground. Hanging from it were several shanks of raw meat. The searchers stared, then cautiously approached it.

'What's this?' Threepio said what all of them were thinking.

Chewie held himself back for as long as he could, but was finally unable to resist. He reached out for one of the huge chunks of meat.

'No, wait!' shouted Luke.

But it was too late. The moment the meat was pulled from the stake, a huge net sprang up around the whole party, instantly hoisting them high above the ground, in a twisting jumble of arms and legs.

Artoo whistled wildly as the Wookiee bayed his regret. Han dragged a hairy paw from his mouth, spitting fur. 'Great, Chewie. Always thinking of your stomach.'

'Take it easy,' Luke said. 'Let's figure out how we can get out of this thing.' He tried in vain to free his arms. One was locked behind him through the mesh: the other pinned by Threepio's leg. 'Can anyone reach my lightsaber?'

Artoo extended his cutting appendage and began cutting the loops of the net. Meantime, Solo was trying to squeeze his arm past Threepio, to reach the lightsaber hanging from Luke's waist.

Suddenly Artoo cut through the last link, and the entire group crashed out of the net to the ground. As they regained their senses, they saw that they were surrounded by a score of small furry creatures, wearing soft leather hoods: all were brandishing spears.

One came close to Han, pushing a long spear into his face and screeching.

Solo knocked the weapon aside. 'Point that thing somewhere else,' he growled.

A second Ewok became alarmed, and lunged at Han. Again, he deflected the spear, but was cut on the arm in the process. Luke reached for his lightsabre, but a third Ewok ran forward, pushed the more aggressive ones aside, and shrieked at them in a scolding tone. Luke decided to hold his fire.

Wounded and angry, Han started to draw his pistol. Luke stopped him with a look. He was uncertain of these little creatures, but he had a feeling that they were friendly.

The Ewoks swarmed round, confiscating all their weapons. Luke even gave up his lightsaber. Chewie growled suspiciously.

Luke turned to Threepio. 'Can you understand what they are saying?'

Threepio rose from the mesh trap, feeling himself for

dents. 'Oh, my head,' he complained.

At the sight of his fully upright body, the Ewoks began squeaking among themselves, pointing and gesticulating. Threepio spoke to the one who appeared to be the leader.

There was a long exchange between them which Threepio did not translate at once. Then suddenly one of the Ewoks dropped his spear and prostrated himself in front of the shining droid. Immediately, all the others did the same.

Threepio looked at his friends with a slightly embarrassed shrug. 'I could be mistaken. They're using a very primitive dialect,' he said, almost apologetically, 'but I believe they think that I'm some sort of god.'

Chewie and Artoo thought that was very funny. They started barking and whistling hysterically. Chewie had to wipe a tear from his eye.

'Then how about using your divine influence to get us out of here?' Han suggested bitingly.

Threepio drew himself to his full height. 'I beg your pardon, Captain Solo, but that wouldn't be proper,' he said indignantly. 'It's against my programming to impersonate a deity.'

Han moved threateningly towards the droid, his fingers itching to pull a plug. 'Listen, you pile of bolts, if you don't ... ' He got no farther. Fifteen Ewok spears thrust menacingly at his face. 'Just kidding,' he said weakly, backing down.

The procession of Ewoks wound its way slowly into the ever-darkening forest — tiny creatures inching through a giant maze. They seemed at home, turning down each dense corridor with confidence.

They carried their four prisoners on their shoulders, tied to long poles with vines. Behind them, others carried Threepio shoulder-high on a litter of branches in the shape of a throne.

CHAPTER SIX

The starry sky seemed very near to the treetops as Luke and his friends were carried into the Ewok village. Luke wasn't aware that it was a village at first. He thought that the orange sparks of light in the distance were stars.

Then he found himself being hoisted up intricate stairways and hidden ramps *around* the immense trunks: and gradually, the higher they went, the bigger and cracklier the lights became until, when the group was hundreds of feet up in the trees, Luke realized that the lights were bonfires – *among* the treetops.

They were finally taken out onto a rickety walkway, too far from the ground for them to see anything below them. For one bleak moment Luke was afraid that they were simply going to be pitched over the brink. But the Ewoks had something else in mind.

The narrow platform ended midway between two trees. The first creature in line grabbed a long vine, and swung across to the far trunk, which had a large cave-like opening carved into its surface. Vines were quickly tossed back and forth across the chasm, until a kind of lattice was constructed, and Luke found himself being pulled across it on his back, still tied to the wooden poles. He looked down once, into nothingness. It was a frightening sensation.

On the other side, they rested on a shaky, narrow platform until everyone was across. Then the Ewoks dismantled the webbing and proceeded into the tree with their captives. It was totally black inside, but Luke sensed that it was more of a tunnel through the wood than an actual cavern. When they emerged, fifty yards farther on, they were in the village square.

It was a series of wooden platforms, planks and walkways, connecting an extensive cluster of trees. Supported by this scaffolding was a village of huts, constructed of an odd combination of stiffened leather, daub and wattle, with thatched roofs and mud floors. Small camp fires burned before many of the huts. Everywhere, there were hundreds of Ewoks.

Cooks, tanners, guards, grandfathers. Mother Ewoks gathered up squealing babies at the sight of the prisoners and scurried into their huts, or pointed and murmured. Dinner smoke filled the air: minstrels played strange music on hollow logs and windy reeds.

There was a vast blackness below, but here in this tiny village, Luke felt warmth and light, and a special peace.

The captives and their captors stopped before the largest hut. Luke, Chewie and Artoo were leaned, on their poles, against a nearby tree. Han was tied to a spit, and balanced above a pile of kindling that looked suspiciously like a barbecue pit.

Teebo emerged from the large structure. He was slightly bigger than most of the others, and undeniably fiercer. Instead of the leathery hood, he wore a horned animal half-skull on his head, adorned with feathers. He carried a stone hatchet, and walked with a swagger.

He examined the group briefly, then seemed to make a kind of pronouncement. At that, a member of the hunting party stepped forward – Paploo, the mantled

Ewok, who had taken a more protective view towards the prisoners.

Teebo conferred with Paploo for a moment. Their discussion soon turned into a heated disagreement, with Paploo, apparently, taking the Rebels' side. The rest of the tribe watched with great interest, shouting comments or squeaking excitedly.

Threepio, whose throne had been set down in a place of honour near the stake to which Solo was tied, followed the argument with fascination.

Han looked over at Luke with a dubious frown. 'I don't like the look of this.'

Suddenly Lograly came from the large hut, silencing everyone with his presence. Shorter than Teebo, he was nonetheless an object of great respect. He, too, wore a half-skull on his head, with a single feather tied to its crest. He carried no weapon: only a pouch at his side, and a staff topped by the spine of a once-powerful enemy.

He looked over the captives, one by one, smelling Han, testing the fabric of Luke's clothing with his fingers. When he came to Chewbacca, he became fascinated and poked the Wookiee with his staff of bones. Chewie took exception to this and growled dangerously. Logray did a quick back step, at the same time reaching into his pouch and sprinkling some herbs in Chewie's direction.

'Careful, Chewie,' Han cautioned from across the square. 'He must be the top man.'

'No,' Threepio corrected him. 'Actually, he's their medicine man.'

Luke was about to intervene but he decided to wait and let the little community draw its own conclusions about them.

Logray wandered over to examine Artoo. He

sniffed, tapped and stroked the little droid's shell, then ordered him to be cut down. Artoo's binders were slashed by two guards and he crashed unceremoniously to the ground.

The guards set him upright, but Artoo was furious. He zeroed in on Teebo and, beeping a blue streak, began to chase the terrified Ewok in circles. Finally, he was close enough to zing him with an electric charge. The shocked Ewok jumped high into the air.

Threepio was furious. 'Artoo, stop that! You're only making matters worse.'

Luke was afraid the situation was getting out of control. 'Threepio, I think it's time you spoke up on our behalf,' he called.

Threepio turned to the assembly of small creatures and made a short speech, pointing from time to time at his captive friends.

His words annoyed Logray. He waved his staff, stamped his feet, and shrieked at the golden droid for a full minute. As he finished, he nodded to several of his fellows who began filling the pit beneath Han with firewood.

'What did he say?' Han shouted with some concern.

Threepio wilted. 'I'm rather embarrassed, Captain Solo, but it appears that you are to be the main course at a banquet in my honour.'

Before Han could protest, log drums began beating. As one, all the furry heads turned towards the door of the large hut. Out of it came Wicket, followed by Chief Chirpa.

On his head, Chirpa wore a garland of woven leaves, teeth and the horns of great animals he had killed in the hunt. In his right hand, he carried a staff fashioned from the longbone of a flying reptile: in his left, he held an iguana, who was his pet and adviser.

He surveyed the scene in the square at a glance, then turned to wait for the guest who was only now emerging from the large hut behind him.

The guest was the beautiful young Princess of Alderaan.

'Leia!' shouted Luke and Han together.

With a gasp, she rushed towards her friends, but a phalanx of Ewoks blocked her way with spears. She turned to Chief Chirpa, then to her droid interpreter. 'Threepio, tell them these are my friends. They must be set free.'

Threepio looked at Chirpa and Logray, and spoke to them in the Ewok tongue, sounding very polite.

Chirpa and Logray shook their heads. Logray chattered an order to his helpers, who vigorously resumed piling wood under Solo. Han exchanged a helpless look with Leia. 'I have the feeling that didn't do us any good,' he commented.

'Luke, what can we do?' Leia pleaded. She'd expected to be guided back to her ship, not to attend an Ewok banquet where her favourite space pirate was the main course.

'Threepio, tell them that if they don't do as you wish, you'll become angry and use your magic,' Luke ordered.

'Master Luke, what magic?' the droid pleaded.

'Tell them,' Luke insisted. There were times when Threepio could test the patience even of a Jedi.

The droid turned to the large audience and spoke with great dignity. The Ewoks seemed greatly disturbed by his words. They all took several steps back, except for Logray who stepped forward. He shouted something at Threepio that sounded like a challenge.

Luke closed his eyes in absolute concentration.

Threepio began rattling but Luke wasn't listening to the droid. With immense concentration, he was visualizing him ... and slowly Threepio began to rise.

Threepio and the Ewoks realized what was happening at the same moment. The Ewoks drew back in terror from the floating throne. Threepio now began to spin, as if he were on a revolving stool.

Chief Chirpa shouted orders to his cowering subjects. Quickly they ran forward and released the bound prisoners. Luke lowered the golden droid gently to the ground. 'Thanks, Threepio.' The young Jedi patted him gratefully on the shoulder.

Threepio, still shaken, stood with a wobbly, amazed smile. 'Why ... why, I didn't know I had it in me.'

Chief Chirpa's hut was large by Ewok standards, though Chewie, sitting cross-legged, nearly scraped the ceiling with his head. He hunched along one side of the dwelling with his Rebel comrades, while the Chief and ten Elders sat on the other side, facing them. Outside, the entire village awaited the Council's decisions.

Threepio was speaking. He was telling an animated history of the Galactic Civil War: at one point, mimicking an Imperial walker.

The Ewok Elders listened carefully, occasionally murmuring comments to each other. It was a fascinating story and they were thoroughly absorbed – at times, horrified and outraged. Logray conferred with Chirpa once or twice, and several times asked Threepio questions, to which the golden droid responded movingly.

In the end, after a brief discussion with the Elders, the Chief shook his head and spoke. Threepio translated his words. 'Chief Chirpa says that it's a very moving story, but it really has nothing to do with the

Ewoks.'

It was finally Han Solo who spoke for the group ... for the Alliance. 'Tell them this, Threepio,' he said. 'They shouldn't help because we're asking them to, nor even because it's in their interest to. I used to do things because they were in *my* interest, but not any more. I do things now for my *friends*, because nothing else is so important. Your friends are ... well, your *friends*. Right?'

His earnest plea brought tears to Leia's eyes, but the Ewoks remained silent and impassive, their expressions unreadable.

After a long pause, Luke began to speak. 'It's terribly important for the entire galaxy that our Rebel force destroys the Imperial presence here on Endor. Look up there, through the smoke hole in the roof. You can count a hundred stars. In the whole sky there are millions more that you can't even see. All of them have planets and moons, and happy people ... just like you. You are part of the beauty: you are part of the Force. And the Empire is trying to destroy it all.'

It took Threepio a while to translate this. He wanted to get the words exactly right. When he finished, there was extensive squeaking among the Elders.

The debate wound down, leaving another moment of quiet. Leia knew what Luke had tried to say, but she feared that the Ewoks did not understand. With an air of confident serenity, she made her appeal. 'Do it because of the trees.' That was all she said.

Wicket had been observing these proceedings with increasing concern. Now he jumped to his feet, paced the width of the hut several times, then began his own impassioned plea. Threepio translated his words.

'Honourable Elders, we have this night received a wondrous gift ... the gift of freedom. This golden god

... ' Here Threepio paused long enough for his friends to realize that the Ewok was talking about him. 'This golden god whose return to us has been prophecied since the First Tree, tells us now that he will not be our master ... that we must *choose* ... as all living creatures must choose their own destiny.

'His friends tell us of a Force, a great living spirit which is now in danger, here and everywhere. When the fire reaches the forest, who is safe? All are in peril.

'It is a brave thing to confront such a fire, Honourable Elders. Many will die so that the forest may live on. And we Ewoks *are* brave.'

The little creature fixed his gaze on the Elders. After a brief pause which gave them time to think, he concluded his statement. 'Honourable Elders, we must aid this noble party.'

He stood before them, the fire still burning in his eyes. The Elders were moved. Without another word, they nodded in agreement. Chief Chirpa rose and announced their decision. The Ewoks were with them.

At once, drums beat throughout the village. The Elders ran across the hut to hug the Rebels. Teebo even hugged Artoo, then hurried across to hop playfully onto Chewie's back.

Han Solo smiled uncertainly. 'What's going on?'

Threepio finally nodded his understanding to Wicket. He turned to the Rebels. 'We are now part of the tribe. The Chief has vowed to help us in any way to rid their land of the evil ones.' He paused. 'His scouts will show us the fastest way to the shield generator.'

Chewie let out a bark, happy to be on the move again. One of the Ewoks thought that he was asking for food and brought him a large chunk of meat. To the Ewoks' amazement, he downed it in a single gulp.

Solo began to organize the expedition. 'How far is

it?' he asked. 'There's not much time, you know.'

During the commotion, Luke drifted to the back of the hut. He avoided the great party which was going on in the square and wandered away from the bonfires to a secluded walkway on the dark side of a colossal tree. Leia followed him.

Luke stared up at the brightest star in the heavens ... the Death Star. He couldn't keep his eyes from it. Leia came to his side. 'What's wrong?' she whispered.

Luke smiled wearily. 'Everything or nothing,' he replied. 'Maybe things are going to be the way they were meant to be.' He felt the presence of Darth Vader very near.

She took his hand. He seemed so lost ... so alone. 'What is it, Luke?'

He looked down at their intertwined fingers. 'Leia, do you remember your mother? Your real mother?'

His question took her by surprise. Flashes from her infancy came back to her. She had lost her mother, and then the Empire had killed her father, and all of her family and friends. Darth Vader and the first Death Star had blown up her entire world. 'Just a little bit,' she replied to him. 'She died when I was very young.'

He turned away, peering up at the Death Star again. 'I have no memory of my mother.'

'Luke, please tell me what's troubling you,' she begged.

He stared at her for a moment. She was strong and he could depend on her. 'Vader is here ... now. On this moon.'

Her blood ran cold. 'How do you know?'

'I can feel his presence. He has come for me.'

'But how could he know that you're here?' she protested.

'He can feel when I am near. As long as I am here, I

81

endanger the whole group and our mission.' His hands trembled. 'I have to face Vader.'

Leia was fast becoming confused. 'I don't understand, Luke. Why do you have to face Vader?'

He drew her close to him, his manner suddenly gentle. 'Darth Vader is my father, Leia.'

'Your father?' she echoed.

Slowly, haltingly, he told her all he had learned from Yoda and Ben Kenobi, then of his last encounter with the Dark Lord which had cost him his hand. He told her too of his belief that the dark side had not claimed Vader completely. 'You see? I must go back to him.'

Leia rose. 'No, Luke. Run away. Far away. If he can feel your presence here, leave this place.'

'We have to fulfil our destinies,' he said, choked.

'But why?' she persisted.

Luke thought of many reasons, but he knew that in the end there was only one, now and always. 'There's good in him. I've felt it. He won't give me over to the Emperor.'

She was crying when suddenly Han stepped up and embraced her from behind. He'd come looking for her, and heard her voice. He arrived just in time to see Luke leaving. But only now did he realize that she was crying.

His smile turned to concern and he asked her what was wrong.

She stifled her sobs and wiped her eyes. 'It's nothing. I just want to be on my own for a while.'

It was plain that she was hiding something. He shook her. 'I want to know what's going on.'

'I can't tell you, Han.' Her lip began to tremble again.

'You can't tell *me*? I thought we were closer than

that, but I guess I was wrong. Maybe you'd rather tell Luke. Sometimes I ...'

'Oh Han,' she cried, burying herself in his embrace. 'Please ... just hold me.' She didn't want to talk but only to be in the comfort of his arms.

Morning mist rose off dewy vegetation as the sun rose over Endor. The lush green foliage had a moist green odour, and in that moment of dawn, the world was silent, as if holding its breath.

In violent contrast, the Imperial landing platform squatted over the ground, harsh, metallic, octagonal. The bushes at its perimeter were charred black from repeated shuttle landings: beyond, the flora was wilting, dying from refuse disposal, trampling feet, chemical exhaust fumes.

Uniformed troops walked continuously on the platform and around the area — loading, unloading, guarding. Imperial walkers were parked to one side — square, armoured, two-legged war machines, large enough for a squad of soldiers to stand inside, firing laser cannons in every direction.

An Imperial shuttle took off for the Death Star. Another walker emerged from the forest on the far side of the platform, returning from a patrol mission. Step by lumbering step, it approached the loading dock.

Darth Vader stood at the rail of the lower deck, staring mutely into the depths of the forest. Like a drum getting louder, he could feel his destiny approaching. He purred in the pit of his throat, like a wild cat sensing game.

The Imperial walker docked at the opposite end of the dock, and opened its doors. A phalanx of stormtroopers filed out in tight formation and marched towards Vader.

Vader turned to face them, his breathing steady, his black robes hanging still in the windless morning. The stormtroopers stopped as they reached him and, at a command from their captain, parted to reveal a bound prisoner in their midst. It was Luke Skywalker.

The young Jedi gazed at Vader with complete calm.

The captain addressed Lord Vader. 'This is the Rebel who surrendered to us. Although he denies it, I believe there are more of them. I request permission to conduct a search of the area.' He extended his hand to the Dark Lord and handed him Luke's lightsaber. 'He was armed only with this.'

Vader looked at the lightsaber for a moment, then took it. 'Conduct your search, and bring his companions to me.'

Luke and Vader were left alone, facing each other in the emerald tranquillity of the ageless forest. The mist was beginning to clear. A long day lay ahead.

CHAPTER SEVEN

'So,' the Dark Lord rumbled, 'you have come to me.'

'And you to me.'

'The Emperor is expecting you. He believes that you will turn to the dark side.'

'I know ... Father.' It was a momentous effort for Luke to address Darth Vader this way. But now that he had done it, he felt stronger.

'So you have finally accepted the truth,' Vader gloated.

'I have accepted the fact that you were once Anakin Skywalker, my father.'

'That name no longer has meaning for me.'

'It is the name of your true self.' Luke's gaze bored steadily at the cloaked figure. 'You have only forgotten. I know that there is good in you. The Emperor hasn't driven it away completely. That's why you could not destroy me. That's why you won't take me to your Emperor now.'

Vader seemed almost to smile through his mask at his son's use of Jedi inner strength. He looked down at the lightsaber the captain had given him — Luke's lightsaber. He held it up. 'So you have constructed another?'

'This is mine,' Luke said quietly. 'I no longer use yours.'

Vader ignited the blade, examining it like an admiring craftsman. 'Your skills are complete. Indeed, you are as powerful as the Emperor has foreseen.'

They stood in silence for a moment, the lightsaber between them.

'Come with me, father.'

Vader shook his head. 'Ben once thought as you do ...'

'Don't blame Ben for your fall ... ' Luke took a step closer then stopped.

Vader did not move. 'You don't know the power of the dark side. I must obey my master.'

'I will not turn. You will be forced to destroy me.'

'If that is your destiny.' This was not Vader's wish but, if necessary, he would destroy Luke. He could not afford to hold back as he had once before.

'Search your feelings, father. You can't do this. I feel the conflict within you. Let go of your hatred.'

'Someone has filled your mind with foolish ideas, young one. The Emperor will show you the true nature of the Force. *He* is your master now.'

Luke and the Dark Lord faced each other for another long, searching moment. Vader extinguished Luke's lightsaber and signalled to a squad of distant stormtroopers. 'It is too late for me, Son,' he said, just before the guards arrived.

'Then my father is truly dead,' answered Luke.

The vast Rebel fleet hung poised in space, ready to strike. It was hundreds of light years from the Death Star, but in hyperspace, all time was but a moment. The deadliness of attack was not measured in distance, but in precision.

The calculations required to launch such an offensive at the speed of light made it necessary to fix on a stationary point. The point chosen by the Rebel command was a small blue planet of the Sullust system. The armada was positioned around it now.

The *Millenium Falcon* finished its round of the fleet's perimeter, checking final positions, then pulled into space beneath the flagship. The time had come.

Lando was at the *Falcon*'s controls. Beside him, his co-pilot Nien Nunb — a jowled mouse-eyed creature from Sullust — flipped switches, monitored readouts and made final preparations for the jump to hyperspace.

Lando set his comlink to war channel. With dry mouth, he made his report to Admiral Ackbar on the command ship. 'Admiral, we're in position. All fighters are accounted for.'

Ackbar's voice crackled back over the headset. 'Proceed with the countdown. All groups assume attack positions.'

Lando turned to his co-pilot with a quick smile. 'Don't worry. My friends are down there. They'll have that shield down in time.' He turned back to his instruments. 'Stand by,' he grunted, patting the control panel for good luck.

On the bridge of the Star Cruiser command ship, Ackbar looked around at his generals. 'Are all groups in their attack positions?' he asked.

'Affirmative, Admiral.'

Ackbar gazed out of his view-window at the starfield, for perhaps the last peaceful moment he would ever know. He spoke finally into the comlink war channel. 'All craft will begin the jump to hyperspace on my mark. May the Force be with us.' He reached forward to the signal button.

In the *Falcon*, Lando stared at the galactic ocean with the same sense of excitement and foreboding. They were doing what a guerrilla force should never do — engage the enemy like a traditional army. The Alliance had been drawn into the open to fight the war on the Emperor's terms. If the Rebels lost this battle, they lost the war.

Suddenly, Ackbar's signal light flashed on the control panel. The attack was commenced.

Lando pulled back the conversion switch and opened up the throttle. Outside the cockpit, the stars began streaking by. The streaks grew brighter as the ships of the fleet roared at lightspeed, then soared through the warp into hyperspace.

The blue crystal planet hovered in space, once again alone in the void.

The strike squad crouched behind a woody ridge overlooking the Imperial outpost. Leia viewed the area through a small electronic scanner.

Two shuttles were being offloaded on the landing platform docking ramp. Several walkers were parked nearby. Troops stood around, helped with construction, took watch, carried supplies. The massive shield generator hummed at the side.

Flattened down in the bushes with the strike force were several Ewoks, including Wicket, Teebo and Paploo. The rest stayed lower, behind the knoll and out of sight.

Leia put down the scanner and scuttled back to the others. 'The entrance is on the far side of that landing platform,' she said. 'This isn't going to be easy.'

Chewie barked his agreement.

Han gave the Wookiee a pained look. 'We've gotten into more heavily guarded places than that.'

Suddenly Warwick began chattering and pointing. He gabbled something to Wicket. Threepio translated.

'Apparently Wicket knows a back entrance to this installation.'

Han perked up at that. 'A back door? That's it. That's how we'll do it.'

Four Imperial scouts kept watch over the entrance to the bunker that half emerged from the earth far to the rear of the main section of the shield generator complex. Their speeder bikes were parked nearby.

In the undergrowth beyond, the Rebel strike squad lay in wait.

'With only those guards, this should be easier than breaking a Bantha,' Han mused.

'It only takes one to sound the alarm,' Leia pointed out cautiously.

Han grinned. 'Then we'll have to move real quietly. If Luke can keep Vader off our backs like you said he would, this should be no sweat. Just hit those guards fast and quiet.'

Threepio explained the problem to Teebo. The Ewoks gabbled for a moment, then one of them jumped up and raced through the undergrowth.

Leia checked the instrument on her wrist. 'We're running out of time. The fleet's in hyperspace by now.'

Threepio muttered a question to Teebo, and received a short reply. 'Oh dear,' Threepio fussed. 'I'm afraid one of our furry companions has done something rash.'

'What are you talking about?' Leia demanded.

The Ewok had scampered through the bushes to where the scouts' bikes were parked. Now, the Rebel leaders watched with horror as the little ball of fur swung his pudgy body up onto one of the bikes, and began flipping switches at random. Before anyone could stop him, the bike's engines ignited with a roar.

The four scouts looked over in surprise. The Ewok grinned madly and continued playing with the switches.

'So much for our surprise attack,' Han growled disgustedly.

The Imperial scouts raced towards the Ewok just as the forward drive engaged, wooming him into the forest. His stubby paws could barely control the handlebar. Three of the guards jumped onto their own bikes, and sped off in pursuit. The fourth stayed at his post, near the door of the bunker.

'Not bad for a ball of fuzz,' Han said admiringly. He nodded at Chewie and the two of them slipped down towards the bunker.

Meanwhile, the Ewok was sailing through the trees, more by luck than judgment. It was terrifying, but he loved it.

The Imperial scouts were already pulling in sight of him. When they started firing laser bolts, he finally decided that he'd had enough. As he rounded the next tree, just out of their sight, he grabbed a vine and swung up into the branches. The three scouts tore by underneath him, pressing their pursuit to the limit. He giggled furiously.

Back at the bunker, the remaining scout had been overcome. Sudbued by Chewbacca, bound and stripped, he was being carried into the woods by two other members of the team. The rest of the squad crouched silently around the entrance.

Han stood at the door, checking the stolen code against the digits on the bunker's control panel. He punched a series of buttons and the door opened silently.

Leia peered inside. No sign of life. She beckoned the others and entered the bunker. Han and Chewie were close on her heels. Soon the entire team was huddled inside the steel corridor, leaving one lookout, wearing the unconscious guard's uniform, at the entrance. Han pushed a series of buttons on the inner panel, closing the door behind them.

Leia thought briefly of Luke. She hoped that he could detain Vader for long enough to allow her to destroy the shield generator. She hoped even more that he could avoid a direct confrontation with him, for she feared that Vader was the stronger of the two. Furtively, she led the way down the dark and low-beamed tunnel.

Vader's shuttle settled onto the docking bay of the Death Star like a black, wingless bird. Luke and the Dark Lord emerged with a small escort of stormtroopers, and walked rapidly across the main bay to the Emperor's tower elevator.

Royal guards awaited them, flanking the shaft. They opened the elevator door. Luke stepped forward. He hoped that Leia would deactivate the deflector shield quickly and destroy the Death Star before anything else happened. He felt that the closer he came to the Emperor, the more something else was likely to happen.

The elevator door opened. Luke and Vader came out alone. They crossed the unlit antechamber and climbed the grating stairs to stand before the throne: father and son, side by side, one masked and one exposed beneath the gaze of the evil Emperor.

Vader bowed to his master. The Emperor motioned him to rise, and smiled graciously at Luke. 'Welcome, young Skywalker. I have been expecting you.'

Luke stared defiantly at the bent, hooded figure.

The Emperor's smile grew softer, fatherly even. He

glanced at Luke's manacles. 'You no longer need these,' he said. He made the slightest movement with his finger in the direction of Luke's wrists and immediately the binders fell away, clattering to the floor.

Luke looked at his hands – now free to reach out for the Emperor's throat ... to crush his windpipe in an instant.

Yet the Emperor seemed gentle. Had he not just let Luke free? But Luke knew that he was devious, too. Do not be fooled by appearances, Ben had told him. Luke continued to stare at his freed hands. He could end it right there ... or could he? He had total freedom of choice, yet he could not choose.

The Emperor sat before him smiling. 'Tell me, young Skywalker,' he said, sensing Luke's indecision. 'Who has been involved in your training until now?'

Luke remained silent. He would reveal nothing.

'I know it was Obi-Wan Kenobi at first,' the Emperor continued, rubbing his hands together. 'Of course, we are familiar with the talent Obi-Wan Kenobi had when it came to training Jedi.' He nodded at Vader, Obi-Wan's previous star pupil.

Luke tensed at the Emperor's sneer, but he tried to keep his anger under control, for losing his calm was playing into the Emperor's hands.

Palpatine noted the emotion on Luke's face, and chuckled. 'So, in your early training you have followed your father's path, it would seem. But, alas, Obi-Wan is now dead, I believe. His elder student here saw to that.' Again he nodded at Vader. 'So, tell me, who continued your training?'

Luke kept silent, struggling to maintain his composure.

The Emperor drummed his fingers on the arm of the

throne. 'There was one called ... Yoda, an aged master Jedi. Ah, I see by your expression that I have hit a chord. Yoda, then?'

Luke flushed with anger at himself for revealing so much. He strove to calm himself – to see all, but to show nothing.

He focused on the emptiness of space beyond the window. He filled his mind with this blackness.

'Very good, young Skywalker. You almost hid this from me, but you could not and you cannot. This is my first lesson to you,' the Emperor beamed.

Luke wilted for a moment, yet in the very faltering, he found strength. Ben and Yoda both instructed him to fall when attacked and then to rise again.

The Emperor watched Luke's face with cunning. 'I'm sure that Yoda taught you to use the Force with great skill?'

Vader saw the Emperor lick his lips at the sight of Luke's uncertain reaction, and heard him laugh from the back of his throat.

Luke paused, for he saw something else, something he had not seen in the Emperor before ... fear.

In his heart, the Emperor feared that Luke's power could be turned on him, just as Vader had turned his on Obi-Wan Kenobi. Luke knew now that the odds had shifted slightly.

With absolute calm, Luke stood upright. He stared directly into the evil ruler's hood. Palpatine said nothing for a few moments, but returned the young Jedi's gaze, assessing his strengths and weaknesses. Eventually, he sank back. 'I look forward to completing your training, young Skywalker. In time, you will call *me* Master.'

For the first time, Luke felt steady enough to answer him back. 'You are gravely mistaken. You will not convert me as you did my father.'

Palpatine leapt to his feet. He came down from the throne and stared venomously into the boy's eyes. At last, Luke saw the entire face within the hood: eyes sunken like tombs, the flesh decayed beneath the skin, the breath, corrupt.

Vader extended a gloved hand holding Luke's lightsaber to the Emperor. The Emperor took it slowly and walked with it across the room to the huge circular view-window. The Death Star had been revolving slowly, so the Sanctuary Moon was now visible. He looked at Endor and then at the lightsaber in his hand. 'Ah yes, a Jedi's weapon, much like your father's.' He faced Luke directly. 'By now you must know that your father can never be turned from the dark side. So will it be with you.'

'Never,' Luke vowed. 'Soon I will die, and you with me.'

The Emperor laughed cynically. 'Perhaps you refer to the imminent attack of your Rebel fleet? I assure you that we are quite safe from your friends here.'

Vader walked to the Emperor's side, also staring at Luke.

Luke felt increasingly inexperienced. 'Your over-confidence is your weakness,' he challenged them.

'And your faith in your friends is yours,' the Emperor retorted, his voice growing angry. 'Everything that has happened has been by *my* design. Your friends up there are walking into a trap, and so is your Rebel fleet.'

Luke's face began to twitch nervously. The Emperor chuckled with malicious glee. 'It was *I* who allowed the Alliance to know the location of the shield generator. An entire Legion of my troops awaits your friends there.'

Luke's eyes darted from the Emperor to Vader, and finally to the lightsaber in the Emperor's hand. He could rely on nothing and nobody but himself.

The Emperor continued imperiously, 'I'm afraid the deflector shield will be quite operational when your fleet arrives. And that is only the beginning of my surprise ... but I don't wish to spoil it for you.'

The situation was degenerating fast for Luke. Defeat after defeat was being piled upon his head. There seemed no end to the evil deeds Palpatine could inflict upon the galaxy. Luke raised his hand in the direction of the lightsabre.

'From here, young Skywalker, you will witness the final destruction of the Alliance, and the end of your insignificant rebellion,' the Emperor taunted.

Luke raised his hand farther. He realized that both Palpatine and Vader were watching him, and tried to recover his earlier calm so that he could decide what to do.

The Emperor smiled thinly. He offered the lightsaber to Luke. 'You want this, don't you? The hate is swelling in you. Very good, take it. Use it. I am unarmed. Give in to your anger. With every passing moment you make yourself more my servant.'

Luke tried to hide his inner agony. 'No, never!' He thought desperately of Ben and Yoda. They were part of the Force now. Was it possible for them to distort the Emperor's vision by their presence? No one was infallible, Ben once told him. Surely the Emperor could not foresee everything? *Ben*, thought Luke, *if ever I needed your guidance it is now*.

The Emperor leered and lay the lightsabre down on the control chair near Luke's hand. 'It is your destiny,' he said quietly. 'You, like your father, are now mine.'

Luke had never felt so lost.

Han, Chewie, Leia and a dozen commandos made their way down the maze of corridors towards the area where the shield generator was marked on the stolen map. Yellow lights illuminated the low rafters, casting long shadows at each intersection. At the first three turnings, all remained quiet. They saw no guards nor workers.

At the fourth intersection, six Imperial storm-troopers stood guard. There was no way round them. The intersection had to be crossed. Han and Leia exchanged a glance. They had no alternative but to fight.

With pistols drawn, they charged into the entry. Almost as if they'd been expecting an attack, the guards instantly crouched and began firing their weapons. A barrage of laser bolts followed, bouncing from girder to floor. Two stormtroopers were killed instantly. A third lost his gun and was pinned behind a refrigerator console.

Two more stood in the back of a fire door, and blasted each commando as he tried to get through. Four went down. The guards were almost impregnable behind their vulcanite shields ... but *almost* didn't account for Wookiees.

Chewbacca rushed the door, dislodging it on top of the two stormtroopers and crushing them. Leia shot the sixth guard as he stood to draw a bead on Chewie. The trooper who'd been crouched beneath the refrigerator suddenly bolted to go for help. Han raced after him and brought him down with a flying tackle.

They checked their numbers. Their casualties were not too bad. But now they had to hurry before a general alarm was raised. The power centre that was their target was very near. There would be no second chances.

The Rebel fleet broke out of hyperspace with an awesome roar. Amidst glistening streamers of light, battalion after battalion emerged in formation to fire off towards the Death Star and its Sanctuary Moon, hovering brightly in the close distance. Soon the entire navy, led by the *Millenium Falcon*, was bearing down on its target.

Lando was worried from the moment they came out of hyperspace. 'We must be able to get some kind of reading on the shield,' he muttered.

Nien Nunb pointed to the control panel.

'Jammed? How can they be jamming us if they don't know we're coming?' Lando grimaced at the oncoming Death Star as the grim truth dawned on him. This was not a surprise attack after all. They had been lured into a trap.

He hit the switch on his comlink. 'Break off the attack! The shield is still up!'

Red Leader's voice shouted back over the headset. 'I get no reading. Are you sure?'

'Pull up!' Lando commanded. 'All craft pull up!'

He banked hard to his left, the fighters of Red Squad veering close on his tail. Some didn't make it. Three flanking X-wings nicked the invisible deflector shield, spinning out of control and exploding in flames along the shield's surface.

On the Rebel Star Cruiser bridge, alarms were screaming, lights flashing, klaxons blaring, as the mammoth space cruiser abruptly tried to change course in time to avoid collision with the shield. Officers were running from battle stations to navigation controls.

Admiral Ackbar spoke urgently but quietly into his comlink. 'Take evasive action,' he ordered. 'Green Group steer course for Holding Sector. MG-7 Blue

Group.'

A Calamari controller, across the bridge, called out to Ackbar. 'Admiral, we have enemy ships at Sectors RT-23 and PB-4.'

The large central viewscreen no longer showed just the Death Star and the green moon behind it, floating isolated in space. Now the vast Imperial fleet could be seen, flying in perfect formation, out from behind Endor, in two gigantic flanking waves – heading to surround the Rebel fleet from both sides, pincers of a deadly scorpion. And the shield blocked the Alliance fleet in front.

Ackbar spoke desperately into his comlink. 'It's a trap. Prepare for attack.'

An anonymous fighter pilot's voice came back over the radio. 'Fighters coming in! Here we go!'

The attack began.

TIE fighters first – they were much faster than the bulky Imperial cruisers, so they were the first to make contact with the Rebel invaders. Savage dog-fights ensued, and soon the black sky was aglow with explosions.

An aide approached Ackbar. 'We've added power to the forward shield, Admiral.'

'Good. Double power on the main battery, and ... ' The Star Cruiser was rocked by the fireworks outside.

'Gold Wing is hit hard,' another officer shouted, stumbling onto the bridge.

'Give them cover,' Ackbar shouted. 'We must make extra time.' As he spoke into the comlink, yet another explosion rocked the frigate. 'All ships stand your position. Wait for my command to return.'

It was far too late for Lando and his attack squadrons to heed this order. They were already way ahead of the pack, heading straight for the oncoming

Imperial fleet.

Wedge Antilles, Luke's old comrade from the first campaign, led the X-wings that accompanied the *Falcon*. As they drew near the Imperial defenders, his voice came over the comlink, calm and experienced. 'Lock X-foils in attack position.'

The wings opened like dragonflies, poised for increased manoeuvering.

'All wings report in,' called Lando.

'Red Leader standing by,' Wedge replied.

'Green Leader standing by.'

'Blue Leader standing by.'

'Grey leader ...'

The last transmission was interrupted by an explosion that disintegrated Grey Wing entirely.

'Here they come,' Wedge muttered.

'Accelerate to attack speed,' Lando ordered. 'Draw fire away from our cruisers for as long as possible.'

'Copy, Gold Leader,' Wedge responded. 'We're moving to point three across the axis ...'

'Two of them are coming in at twenty degrees,' somebody warned.

'I see them,' noted Wedge. 'Cut left. I'll take the leader.'

'Watch yourself, Wedge. Three from above ...'

'Yeah, I ...'

'I'm on it, Red Leader.'

'There are too many of them.'

'Red four, watch out!'

'I'm hit!' The X-wing spun across the starfield into the void.

'Red six, a squadron of fighters has broken through.'

'They're heading for the medical frigate. After them!'

'Go ahead,' Lando agreed. 'I'm going in. There are

four marks at point three five. Cover me.'

'Right behind you, Gold Leader.'

'Hang on, back there.'

'Close up formations, Blue Group.'

'Good shooting, Red two.'

Lando steered the *Falcon* into a complete flip, as his crew fired at the Imperial fighters from the belly guns. Two were direct hits: the third a glancing blow that caused a TIE fighter to crash into one of its companions. The *Falcon* was faster by half than anything else that flew.

Within minutes, the battlefield was a bright red glow, spotted with puffs of smoke, blazing fireballs, whirling spark showers, spinning debris, shafts of light, tumbling machinery, space-frozen corpses.

Nien Nunb made a guttural remark to Lando.

'You're right,' the pilot agreed. 'Only their fighters are attacking. What are those star destroyers waiting for?' It looked as though the Emperor had another trick up his sleeve. He glanced at Endor, floating peacefully in space, to his right. 'Come on, Han, don't let me down.'

Han pressed the button on his wrist unit and covered his head. The reinforced door to the main control room blew into melted pieces, and the Rebel squad stormed through.

The stormtroopers inside were taken completely by surprise. A few were injured by the exploding door: the rest gaped in dismay as the Rebels rushed them with guns drawn. Han took the lead, with Leia right behind him, and Chewie at the rear.

They herded the troopers into a corner of the bunker. Three commandos guarded them: three more covered the exits. The rest began placing the explosive charges.

Leia studied one of the screens on the control panel. 'Hurry, Han! The fleet is being attacked.'

Han looked over at the screen. 'Blast it! With the shield still up, their backs are against the wall.'

'That is correct,' came a voice from the rear of the room. 'Just as *yours* are.'

Han and Leia spun round to find dozens of Imperial guns trained on them. An entire legion had been hiding in the wall compartments of the bunker. Now the Rebels were surrounded, with nowhere to run and far too many stormtroopers for them to put up a fight.

More Imperial troops charged through the door, roughly disarming the stunned commandos. Han, Chewie and Leia exchanged hopeless glances. They had been the Rebellion's last chance.

And they had failed.

Some distance from the main battle area, in the centre of the blanket of ships which comprised the Imperial fleet, was the flag ship, Super Star Destroyer. On the bridge, Admiral Piett watched the war through the enormous observation window.

Two fleet captains stood beside him, respectfully silent. 'Have the fleet held here,' Piett ordered.

The first officer hurried to carry out the order. The second spoke to the Admiral. 'Aren't we going to attack?' he asked.

Piett smirked. 'I have my orders from the Emperor himself. He has something special planned for this Rebel scum. We are only to keep them from escaping.'

The Emperor, Lord Vader and Luke watched the aerial battle from the safety of the Death Star's throne room. Luke looked on with horror as one Rebel ship then another toppled against the invisible deflector shield and exploded.

Vader watched Luke. His son was powerful, stronger than he had imagined ... and not lost yet either to the Force or to the Emperor. There was still time for him to take Luke for himself, to join with him in dark majesty and for them to rule the galaxy together. It would take only patience and a little wizardry to show Luke the advantages of the dark way, and prise him from the Emperor's clutches.

Vader knew, too, that Luke had sensed the Emperor's fear. He's a clever boy, young Luke, Vader thought, his father's son.

The Emperor interrupted Vader's thoughts with a cackled remark to Luke. 'As you can see, my young apprentice, the deflector shield is still in place. Your friends have failed. And now ... ' He raised his spindly hand. ' ... witness the power of this fully armed and operational battle station.' He walked across to the comlink. 'Fire at will, Commander,' he ordered.

Shocked, Luke looked out across the surface of the Death Star to the battlefield beyond, and to the bulk of the Rebel fleet beyond that.

In the bowels of the Death Star, Commander Jerjerrod gave an order. A controller pulled a switch which ignited a blinking panel. Two hodded Imperial soldiers pressed a series of buttons. A thick beam of light slowly pulsed from a heavily blockaded shaft. On the outer surface of the completed half of the Death Star, a giant laser dish began to glow.

Luke watched in horror as the beam radiated from the muzzle of the Death Star. It touched one of the Rebel Star Cruisers that was surging in the midst of the heaviest fighting. Instantly, the Star Cruiser was vaporized.

In the numbing grip of despair, Luke's eyes glinted, for again he saw his lightsaber, lying unattended on the throne. In this bleak moment, the dark side was much with him.

CHAPTER EIGHT

Admiral Ackbar stood on the bridge in stunned disbelief, looking out of the observation window at the place where, only a moment before, the Rebel Star Cruiser *Liberty* had been engaged in a furious long-range battle. Now there was nothing but empty space, powdered with a fine dust that sparkled in the light of more distant explosions.

Around him, confusion was rampant. Flustered controllers were still trying to contact *Liberty*, while fleet captains ran from screen to port, shouting, directing, misdirecting.

An aide handed Ackbar the comlink. General Calrissian's voice was coming through. 'Home-one, this is Gold Leader. That blast came from the Death Star! Repeat ... the Death Star is operational!'

'We saw it,' Ackbar answered wearily. 'All craft prepare to retreat.'

'I refuse to give up and run,' Lando shouted back.

'We have no choice, General. Our cruisers can't repel that sort of fire power.'

'You won't get a second chance, Admiral. Han will still get that shield down. We have to give him more time. Head for those Star Destroyers.'

Ackbar looked round him. A huge charge of flack rumbled against the ship, painting a brief waxen light over the window. Calrissian was right. There would be no second chance. It was now or never. He turned to his captain. 'Move the fleet forward.'

The captain paused. 'Sir, we don't stand much of a chance against those Star Destroyers. They out-gun us, and they're much more heavily armoured.'

'I know,' Ackbar agreed.

An aide approached. 'Forward ships have made contact with the Imperial fleet, Admiral.'

'Concentrate your fire on their power generators. If we can knock out that shield, our fighters might stand a chance against them.'

The ship was rocked by another explosion. A laser bolt hit one of the aft gyro-stabilizers.

'Intensify auxilliary shields!' someone yelled.

The pitch of the battle soared higher.

Beyond the window of the throne room, the Rebel fleet was being decimated in the soundless vacuum of space. Inside, the only sound was the Emperor's throaty cackle. Luke grew more desperate with every minute as the Death Star's laser beam incinerated ship after ship.

'Your fleet is lost ... and your friends on Endor will not survive,' the Emperor hissed. He pushed a comlink button on the arm of his throne, and spoke into it with relish. 'Commander Jerjerrod, if the Rebels manage to blow up the shield generator, you will turn this battle station onto the Endor moon and destroy it.'

'Yes, Your Highess,' Jerjerrod's voice replied, 'but we have several battalions stationed on ...'

'You will destroy it!' The Emperor's whisper was more sinister than any scream.

Palpatine turned back to Luke. 'There is no escape, my young pupil. The Alliance will die ... as will your friends.'

Vader watched Luke's anguished expression, as did the Emperor. The lightsaber began to shake in its resting place. The young Jedi's hand was trembling, his lips pulled back in grimace, his teeth grinding.

The Emperor smiled. 'Good. I can feel your anger. Take your weapon. Strike me down with all your hatred, and your journey towards the dark side will be complete.' He began to laugh incontrollably.

Luke could resist no longer. The lightsaber rattled more violently for a moment on the throne, then flew to his hand, impelled by the Force. He ignited it and fiercely swung it with his full weight down towards the Emperor's skull.

In that moment, Vader's blade flashed into view, parrying Luke's sword an inch above the Emperor's head. Sparks flew like forging steel, bathing Palpatine's grinning face in a hellish glare.

Luke jumped back and turned, lightsaber upraised, to face his father. Vader extended his own blade, poised to fight him. The Emperor sighed with pleasure and sat back on his throne, the sole witness to this dire contest.

Han, Leia, Chewbacca and the rest of the strike team were escorted out of the bunker by their captors. The clearing outside was now filled with Imperial troops, hundreds of them, in white or black armour. Some were viewing the scene from their two-legged walkers, others leaning on their speeder bikes.

Han and Leia turned to each other. All they'd struggled for had failed. The end seemed near. There was so much to say, but they couldn't find a single word. Instead, they simply joined hands for these final minutes of companionship.

This was when Threepio and Artoo jauntily entered the clearing, jabbering and bleeping excitedly to each other. They stopped dead in their tracks when they saw what the clearing had become. 'Oh dear,' Threepio whimpered. Immediately, he and Artoo turned and ran back into the woods.

Six Imperial stormtroopers charged in after them and were in time to see the two droids duck behind a large tree, just a little way into the forest. As they rounded the tree, they found Threepio and Artoo waiting quietly to be taken.

The guards moved towards them, but they moved too slowly. Fifteen Ewoks jumped from the over-hanging branches, quickly overpowering the Imperial troops with rocks and clubs. At that, Teebo — perched in another tree — raised a ram's horn to his lips, and sounded three long blasts. That was the signal for the Ewoks to attack.

Hundreds of them descended upon the clearing from all directions, throwing themselves against the might of the Imperial army with unrestrained zeal. The scene was unbridled chaos.

Stormtroopers fired their laser pistols at the furry creatures, killing or wounding many, only to be attacked by dozens more in their place. Biker scouts chased squealing Ewoks into the woods, and were knocked from their bikes by volleys of rocks launched from the trees.

In the first confused moments of the attack, Chewie dived into the foliage, while Han and Leia hit the dirt in the cover of the arches flanking the bunker door. Explosions all round kept them pinned from moving: the bunker door was closed again, and locked.

Han punched out the stolen code again on the control panel, but this time the door didn't open. It had been reprogrammed as soon as they were caught.

Leia stretched for a laser pistol, lying in the dirt beside a felled stormtrooper. Shots were crisscrossing from every direction.

'We need Artoo,' she shouted.

Han nodded, signalled to the little droid on his comlink, and reached for the weapon that Leia had tried to get.

When Artoo received the message, he and Threepio were huddled behind a tree. Artoo blurted out an excited whistle and shot off towards the battlefield. Threepio, alarmed, followed in his wake.

Biker scouts raced over and around the scurrying droids, still blasting at the Ewoks, who grew fiercer every time their fur was scorched. The little creatures were hanging onto the legs of the Imperial walkers, tripping them with lengths of vine, or injuring their joint mechanisms by forcing pebbles into the hinges. They were knocking more scouts off their bikes by stringing vines between trees at throat level. They were throwing rocks, jumping out of trees, impaling with spears, entangling with nets. They were everywhere.

Several of them rallied behind Chewbacca. He was flinging stormtroopers left and right in a Wookiee frenzy, any time he saw them harming his small friends. For their part, the Ewoks followed Chewie to throw themselves on any soldiers who started getting the better of him.

It was a wild, strange battle.

Han and Leia provided cover with guns they'd finally captured as the two droids finally made it to the bunker door. Artoo moved quickly to the terminal, plugged in his computer arm, and began scanning. A laser bolt ripped the entrance, disengaging Artoo's cable arm, spilling him into the dirt.

His head began to smoulder and his fittings to leak. Every compartment sprung open, every nozzle gushed or smoked, every wheel span ... then stopped. Threepio rushed to his wounded companion as Han examined the bunker terminal.

Meanwhile, the Ewoks had erected a primitive catapult at the other side of the field. They fired a large boulder at one of the walkers. The machine vibrated but it did not fall. It turned and headed for the catapult, laser cannon firing. The Ewoks scattered. When the walker was ten feet away, the Ewoks chopped a mass of vines and two huge trunks crashed down on top of the walker, halting it for good.

The next phase of the assault began. Ewoks in kite-like hang-gliders made from animal skin started dropping rocks on the stormtroopers, and dive-bombing them with spears. Teebo, who led this attack, was hit in the wing with laser fire and crashed into a gnarled root. A charging walker clumped forward to crush him, but Wicket swooped down just in time, yanking Teebo to safety.

And so it went. The casualties mounted.

High above, a thousand deadly dog-fights and cannon bombardments were erupting all over the sky, while the Death Star laser beam methodically disintegrated the Rebel ships.

In the *Millenium Falcon*, Lando steered like a maniac through an obstacle course of floating Imperial Star Destroyers, trading laser bolts with them, dodging flak, and outracing TIE fighters.

Desperately, he was shouting into his comlink, over the noise of explosions, talking to Ackbar in the Alliance command ship. 'I said *closer*. Move in as close as you can and engage the Star Destroyers at close range. That way the Death Star won't be able to fire at us without knocking out its own ships.'

'But no one's ever gone nose to nose at that range between supervessels like their destroyers and our cruisers,' Ackbar protested.

'Great!' yelled Lando. 'Then we're inventing a new form of combat.'

'We won't last long against Star Destroyers at that range.' Ackbar felt giddy with resignation.

'We'll last longer than we will against that Death Star ... and we might as well take a few of them with us,' Lando whooped. One of his forward guns was blown away with a jolt. He put the *Falcon* into a controlled spin, and careered round the belly of the Imperial giant.

With little to lose, Ackbar decided to try Calrissian's strategy. In the next few minutes, dozens of Rebel cruisers moved in close to the Imperial Star Destroyers, and the colossal antagonists began blasting away at each other, while hundreds of tiny fighters raced across their surfaces, zipping between laser bolts as they chased around the massive holds.

Slowly Luke and Vader circled. Lightsaber high above his head, Luke readied his attack from classic first position: the Dark Lord held a lateral stance, in classic answer. Luke brought his blade straight down. Then, when Vader moved to parry, Luke feinted, and cut low. Vader couterparried, let the impact direct his sword towards Luke's throat, but Luke stepped back. Their first blows were traded without injury.

Again they circled. Vader was impressed by the boy's speed. It was a pity he couldn't let him kill the Emperor yet, but Luke wasn't ready for it. There was still a chance that Luke would return to his friends if he killed the Emperor now. He needed more extensive training by both Vader *and* Palaptine, before he'd be ready to take his place at Vader's right hand, ruling the galaxy.

Before Vader could gather his thoughts any further, Luke attacked again — much more aggressively. He advanced in a flurry of lunges, each met with a loud crack by Vader's glowing saber. The Dark Lord retreated a step at every slash, wheeling round once to bring his cutting beam up viciously, but Luke batted it away, pushing Vader back yet again. The Lord of the Sith momentarily lost his footing on the stairs and tumbled to his knees.

Luke stood above him, at the top of the staircase, heady with his own power. He knew that it was in his power now to take Vader ... his blade, his life, his place at the Emperor's side. The choice was his. Then another thought struck him. He could destroy the Emperor, too. Destroy both of them and rule the galaxy.

For the first time, the thought entered Vader's head that his son might best him. He was astounded by the strength Luke had acquired since their last duel, in the Cloud City. The boy's timing was razor sharp. Vader felt humiliation crawling in on his surprise ... and fear. Suddenly his anger rose. He wanted revenge.

The young Jedi's inner turmoil was mirrored in his face. The Emperor saw this and goaded Luke on to revel in his darkness. 'Be at one with your hatred, boy,' he called. 'Let it nourish you!'

Luke faltered for a moment. He was suddenly confused again. He took a step back, lowered his sword, and tried to force the hatred from his being.

In that instant, Vader attacked. He lunged half up the stairs, forcing Luke to reverse defensively. He bound the boy's blade with his own, but Luke disengaged and leapt to the safety of an overhead gantry. Vader jumped over the railing to the floor beneath the platform upon which Luke stood.

'You are unwise to lower your defences,' Vader warned. He wanted Luke to know that this was no longer just a game. This was darkness.

Luke heard something else, though. 'Your thoughts betray you, father. I feel the good in you ... the conflict. You could not bring yourself to kill me before, and you won't destroy me now.'

This accusation *really* made Vader angry. He could tolerate no more from this insolent youth. He must teach him a lesson he would never forget. 'Once again, you underestimate the power of the dark side ...'

Vader flung his glowing blade. It sliced through the supports of the gantry on which Luke was perched, then flew back into Vader's hand. Luke tumbled to the ground, then rolled down to another level, under the tilting platform, until he was out of sight. Vader paced the area like a cat, but he wouldn't enter the shadow of the overhang.

'You cannot hide for ever, Luke.'

'Then come and get me,' Luke challenged him. He put his lightsaber on the ground and rolled it along the floor towards Vader. The Dark Lord held out his hand. Luke's lightsaber flew into it. He hooked it to his belt and, with grave uncertainty, entered the shadowy overhang. 'Give yourself to the dark side, Luke,' he urged. 'It is the only way that you can save your friends.'

Luke withdrew farther into the shadow. Some sixth sense told him that Leia was suffering: her agony cried out to him. 'Never!' he screamed. His lightsaber flew off Vader's belt and into his hand, lighting as it came to

112

him.

He rushed at his father with a frenzy he had never known before. Neither had Vader. They battled fiercely, sparkes flying, but it was soon evident that the advantage was Luke's.

They locked swords, body to body. When Luke pushed Vader back to break the clinch, the Dark Lord hit his head on an overhanging beam. He stumbled backwards. Luke pursued him relentlessly.

Blow upon blow, Luke forced Vader to retreat, back onto the bridge which crossed the vast bottomless shaft to the power core. Each stroke of Luke's saber pummelled the Dark Lord like a scream.

Vader was driven to his knees. He raised his blade to block yet another onslaught, and Luke slashed off his right hand at the wrist. The hand, along with bits of metal, wires and electronic devices, clattered uselessly away while Vader's lightsaber tumbled over the edge, into the endless shaft below.

Luke stared at his father's twitching, severed, mechanical hand, and then at his own black-gloved artificial part. He suddenly realized how much like his father ... the man he hated, he had become.

Trembling, he stood above Vader, the point of his blade at the Dark Lord's throat. He wanted to destroy this thing of darkness, this thing that was once his father, this thing that was ... him.

Suddenly the Emperor was there, looking on and chuckling with uncontrollable delight. 'Good! Kill him!' he gloated. 'Your hate has made you powerful. Now fulfil your destiny and take your father's place at my side.'

Luke hurled his lightsaber away. 'Never! Never will I turn to the dark side. You have failed, Palpatine. I am a Jedi, as my father was before me.'

The Emperor's glee turned to sullen rage. 'So be it, Jedi. If you will not be turned, you will be destroyed.' He raised his spidery arms towards Luke. Blinding white bolts of energy poured from his fingers to shoot across the room like lightning, and tear through the boy's insides as it sought earth.

The young Jedi was confused and in agony. He raised his arms to deflect the bolts, but the shocks came with such speed and power that they coursed through him. He could only shrink before them, convulsed with pain. Slowly, he buckled at the knees.

Vader crawled, like a wounded animal, to his Emperor's side.

On Endor, the battle for the bunker continued. Stormtroopers continued destroying Ewoks with their sophisticated weaponry, but more of the furry little warriors hit back.

They felled trees on their foes. They lured clumsy walkers into branch-covered pits. They started rockslides. They dammed a small stream then opened the floodgates, deluging a host of troops and two more walkers. They jumped on top of walkers from high branches, and poured pouches of burning lizard oil through the gun slits. They used knives, spears and slings, and made frightening war cries to confound their enemy. They were fearless.

Han meanwhile was still working furiously at the control panel. Wires sparked each time he refastened another connection, but still the door would not open. Leia crouched at his back, firing her laser pistol to give him cover.

He motioned her to his side. 'Give me a hand. I think I have it figured out.' He handed her one of the wires. She holstered her weapon, and held it in position as he brought two others from opposite ends of the panel. 'Here goes,' he said.

The three wires sparked: the connection was made. There was a sudden loud roar as a second blast door crashed down in front of the first, doubling the impregnable barrier.

'Great. Now we have two doors to get through,' Leia commented disgustedly.

At that moment, she was hit in the arm by a laser bolt and knocked to the ground.

Han rushed over to her. 'Leia, no!' he cried, trying to stop the bleeding.

'It's not bad,' she shook her head. 'It's —'

'Hold it!' shouted a voice. 'One move and you're both dead!'

They froze. Two stormtroopers stood before them, their weapons levelled. Han and Leia looked at each other, as if to exchange a last goodbye. Then, at an unspoken signal, they whirled out of the stromtroopers' line of fire, and blazed at them with their laser pistols.

As the smoke cleared, a giant Imperial walker lurched onto the scene. It stopped before Han, its laser cannons aimed directly at his face. With a final shattering loss of will, Han dropped his gun and fell to the ground to take Leia in his arms. He was ready to give in.

The hatch at the top of the walker opened and Chewie stuck his head out, barking gleefully at his prank.

Han Solo could have kissed him.

CHAPTER NINE

The two space armadas floated, ship to ship, trading broadsides with each other at point blank range. Some of their deeds were heroic ... suicidal even. One Rebel cruiser, its back alive with fire and explosions, limped into direct contact with an Imperial Star Destroyer, and exploded completely, taking the Star Destroyer with it. Cargo ships loaded with explosives were set on collision courses with fighting vessels, their crews abandoning ships to fates that were uncertain.

Lando, Wedge, Blue Leader and Green Wing went in to take out one of the larger destroyers — the Empire's main communications ship. It had already been damaged by direct fire from the Rebel cruiser it had subsequently destroyed, so now was the time to finish it off.

Lando's squadron went in low, preventing the destroyer from using its bigger guns. It also made the fighter invisible until it was too late for them to be stopped.

'Increase power on the front deflector shields,' Lando ordered his group. 'We're going in.'

They closed up formations and went into a high-speed power dive. Fifty feet from the surface, they pulled out at ninety degrees and raced along the gun metal hull, taking laser fire from every port.

'Start attacking run on the main power tree,' Lando commanded.

'I copy,' answered Green Wing. 'Moving into position.'

'Stay clear of their front batteries,' warned Blue Leader.

'She's badly damaged on the left of the tower,' Wedge noted. 'Concentrate on that side.'

Green Wing was hit. 'I'm losing power!' The pilot took his craft down like a rocket into the destroyer's front batteries. Tremendous explosions wrecked the port bow.

'Thanks,' Blue Leader muttered in admiration.

'That opens it up for us,' Wedge yelled. 'Cut over. The power reactors are just inside that cargo bay.'

'Follow me,' Lando shouted, pulling the *Falcon* into a sharp bank that caught the horrified reactor personnel by surprise. Wedge and Blue followed.

'Direct hit!' Lando whooped.

They pulled up hard and fast as the destroyer became enveloped in a series of ever-increasing explosions, until it finally looked like just one more small star. Blue Leader was caught by a shock wave, and thrown against the side of a smaller Imperial ship, which also exploded. Lando and Wedge escaped.

On the Rebel command ship, smoke and shouts filled the air. Ackbar reached Lando on the comlink. 'The jamming has stopped. We have a reading on the shield.'

'Is it still up?' Lando asked, fearing the worst.

'I'm afraid so. It looks as though General Solo's unit didn't make it.'

'There's still hope until they've destroyed our last ship,' Lando replied. Han wouldn't fail ... he couldn't. They still had to destroy the Death Star.

On the Death Star, Luke was nearly unconscious beneath the onslaught of the Emperor's lightning. Tormented and weakened beyond reason, he wanted nothing more than to surrender to the oblivion towards which he was drifting.

The Emperor smiled down at the enfeebled young Jedi. 'Young fool!' he rasped. 'Only now at the end, do you understand. Your boyish skills are no match for the dark side. Now, young Skywalker, you will pay the price in full. You will die!'

He laughed like a madman and the outpouring of bolts from his outstretched fingers increased in intensity. The sound screamed through the room: the murderous brightness of the flashes was overwhelming.

Luke's body wilted and finally crumpled under the merciless barrage. At last, he appeared totally lifeless. The Emperor hissed maliciously.

At this instant, Darth Vader sprang to his feet and grabbed the Emperor from behind, pinning his upper arms to his torso. Ignoring pain, ignoring his shame and weakness, Vader concentrated solely on his will to defeat the evil embodied in the Emperor.

Palpatine struggled in the wounded Jedi's relentless grip, his fingers still firing bolts of energy in every direction. In his wild flailing, the lightning ripped into Vader, electric currents crackling down his helmet, over his cape and into his heart.

Vader stumbled with his load to the middle of the bridge over the black chasm to the power core. He held the wailing Emperor high above his head and, with a final burst of strength, he pitched him into the abyss.

Palpatine's body, still spewing bolts of light, spun out of control into the void, bouncing back and forth off the sides of the shaft as it fell. It disappeared at last and then, a few seconds later, a distant explosion was heard far down at the core. A rush of air billowed out of the shaft, into the throne room.

The wind whipped Lord Vader's cape, as he staggered towards the hole, trying to follow his master to the end. Luke crawled to his father and pulled him to safety. Both of them lay on the floor, entwined in each other's arms, too weak to move.

Inside the bunker on Endor, Imperial controllers watched the main viewscreen of the Ewok battle outside. The fighting seemed to be winding down.

Suddenly a walker pilot appeared on the screen, waving excitedly. 'It's over, Commander. The Rebels have been routed, and are fleeing with the bear creatures into the woods. We need reinforcements to continue the pursuit.'

'Open the door,' the commander ordered. 'Send three squads to help.'

The bunker door opened and the Imperial troops came rushing out … to find themselves surrounded by Rebels and Ewoks, looking mean and bloody. The Imperial troops surrendered without a fight.

Han, Chewie and five others ran into the bunker with explosive charges. They placed the timed devices at eleven strategic points in and around the power generator, then ran out again as fast as they could.

Leia, still in great pain from her wound, lay in the shelter of some distant bushes. She shouted orders to the Ewoks, to gather their prisoners on the far side of the clearing, away from the bunker. In the next moment, the bunker blew up.

A captain ran to Admiral Ackbar, his voice trembling. 'Sir, the shield around the Death Star has lost its power.'

Ackbar looked at the viewscreen: the electronically generated web had gone. The moon and the Death Star now floated in black, unprotected space. 'They did it,' Ackbar whispered.

He rushed to the comlink and shouted into the multi-frequency war channel. 'All fighters commence attack on the Death Star's main reactor. The deflector shield is down. Repeat. The deflector shield is down.'

Lando's voice was heard. 'I see it. We're on our way. Red group! Gold group! Blue squad! All fighters follow me!'

The *Falcon* plunged to the surface of the Death Star, followed by hordes of Rebel fighters, pursued by a still massing but disorganized array of Imperial TIE fighters. Three Rebel Star Cruisers headed for the huge Imperial Super Star Destroyer, Vader's flagship, which seemed to be having difficulties with its guidance system.

Lando and the first wave of X-wings headed for the unfinished portion of the Death Star, skimming low over the curving surface of the completed side. He turned hard into the unfinished side, and began weaving dangerously among protruding girders, half-built towers, maze-like channels, scaffolding, floodlights.

The anti-aircraft defences weren't well developed here: they'd been depending completely on the protection of the deflector shield. As a result, the Rebel's major sources of worry were the obstructions and the Imperial TIE fighters on their tails.

'I see the power channel system,' Wedge radioed. 'I'm going in.'

'I see it, too,' said Lando. 'Here goes.'

Over a tower and under a bridge ... and suddenly they were flying at top speed inside a deep shaft that was barely wide enough for three fighters, wing to wing. Moreover, it was pierced along its entire twisting length by myriad feeding shafts and tunnels, alternate forks, and dead-end caverns.

A score of Rebel fighters made the first turn-off into the power shaft, followed by twice as many TIEs.

The chase was on.

'Where are we going, Gold Leader?' Wedge called. A laser bolt hit the shaft above him, showering his window with sparks.

'Lock onto the strongest power source,' Lando ordered. 'It should be the generator.'

They quickly strung out into single and double file, as it became apparent that the shaft was not only pocked with side vents and protruding obstacles, but also narrowed across its width at every turn.

TIE fighters hit another Rebel, who exploded in flames. Then another TIE fighter hit a piece of machinery, with a similar result.

'I've got a reading on a major shaft obstruction ahead,' Lando announced.

'Just picked it up,' shouted Wedge. 'Will you make it?'

'It's going to be a tight squeeze.'

The obstruction was a heat-wall blocking three-quarters of the tunnel, with a dip in the shaft to make up a little room. Lando had to spin the *Falcon* through 360 degrees while rising, falling, and accelerating, Luckily, the X-wings and Y-wings weren't quite as bulky but, even so, two more of them didn't make it.

The smaller TIEs drew closer.

Suddenly coarse white static blanketed all the viewscreens. 'My scope's gone,' yelled Wedge.

'Cut speed,' Lando ordered. 'Switch to visual scanning.'

'That's useless at this speed. We'll have to fly nearly blind.'

Two blind X-wings hit the wall as the shaft narrowed again. A third was blown apart by the gaining Imperial fighters.

'Green leader ... ' Lando called. 'Split off and head back to surface. You might draw some fire off us.'

Green Leader and his companion peeled off out of the power shaft, and back up to the cruiser battle. One TIE fighter followed, firing continuously.

Ackbar's voice came over the comlink. 'The Death Star is turning away from the fleet. It looks as though it's repositioning to destroy the Endor Moon.'

'How long before it's in position?' Lando asked.

'Point oh three.'

'That's too soon. We're running out of time.'

Wedge broke into the transmission. 'We're running out of shaft, too,' he called urgently.

At that instant, the *Falcon* scraped through an even narrower opening, damaging her auxilliary thrusters. 'That was too close,' Lando muttered.

Ackbar stared out of the observation window. He was looking down onto the deck of the Super Star Destroyer, now only miles away. Fires burst over its stern, and it was listing heavily to starboard.

'We've knocked out their forward shields,' Ackbar said into the comlink. 'Fire at the bridge.'

Green Leader's group swooped in low, up from the Death Star 'Glad to help out,' Green Leader called.

'Firing proton torpedoes,' Green Wing advised.

The bridge was hit, setting off a rapid chain reaction from power station to power station along the middle third of the huge destroyer, producing a dazzling rainbow of explosions that buckled the ship at right angles, and started it spinning like a pinwheel towards the Death Star.

The first bridge explosion took Green Leader with it: the subsequent uncontrolled joyride snagged ten more fighters, two cruisers and an ordnance vessel. By the time the flaming mass finally crashed into the side of the Death Star, the impact was so tremendous, it jolted the battle station enough to set off internal explosions and thunderings all through its network of reactors, armouries and halls.

The collision with the exploding destroyer was only the beginning, leading to various systems breakdowns which led in turn to reactor meltdowns, personnel panic, abandonment of posts, further malfunctions, and general chaos.

Smoke was everywhere. People were running in every direction and shouting. Electrical fires, steam explosions, cabin depressurizations, disruption of chain-of-command. The continued bombardment by Rebel cruisers heightened the hysteria.

The Emperor was dead. That central, powerful evil which had been the cohesive force of the Empire was gone. The dark side had been reduced to no more than confusion.

Desperation and ... damp fear.

In the midst of this uproar, Luke had somehow made it to the main docking bay, where he was trying to carry the hulking deadweight of his father's weakening body to an Imperial shuttle. Halfway, his strength gave out, and he collapsed under the strain.

He rested his father on the ground, trying to steel himself for a final effort, as the explosions grew louder all around them. Sparks hissed in the rafters, one of the walls buckled, and smoke poured through a gaping fissure. The floor shook.

Darth Vader stirred and sensed the danger that surrounded them. 'Go on, my son,' he whispered urgently. 'Leave me.'

'No,' Luke said. 'I've got to save you.'

'You already have, Luke,' he replied.

Luke shook his head. 'Father, I won't leave you.' The explosions were coming nearer.

Vader pulled him close. 'Luke, help me take off this mask.'

'You'll die,' Luke protested.

'Nothing can stop that now. Just once, let me face you without it. Let me look on you with my own eyes.'

Slowly Luke drew off his father's mask. Beneath it he saw the sad, benign face of an old man, bald, beardless, with a mighty scar running from the top of his head to the back of his scalp. He had unfocussed, deepset dark eyes, and his skin was pasty white, for it had not seen the sun in two decades. The old man smiled weakly; for a moment he looked not too unlike Ben.

'It's too late, Luke, too late!' his father gasped. 'I want to die. I couldn't bear to live on like this in your world. Save yourself!' And Darth Vader, Anakin Skywalker ... Luke's father, died.

A huge explosion shook the Death Star. Luke rose shakily to his feet and stumbled towards a shuttle.

The *Millenium Falcon* continued its swerving race through the maze of power channels, inching ever closer to the hub of the giant sphere – the main reactor. The Rebel cruisers were releasing a continuous bombardment on the exposed superstructure of the Death Star, each hit causing a resonant shudder in the immense battle station, and a new series of catastrophic events within.

Commander Jerjerrod sat, brooding, in the Death Star's control room, watching all about him crumble. Half of his crew were dead or wounded, or had run off in blind panic. The rest wandered in a daze or fired blindly in every direction.

Jerjerrod couldn't fathom what he had done wrong. He'd been patient, loyal, clever and hard. He was the commander of the greatest space station ever built. Or, at least, that was what he believed. Now, however, it seemed that the indestructible was liable to destruction.

Even so, one final duty lay before him. He called for an aide, and hiding his emotion, he beckoned to the aide and barked his instructions.

'Yes, Sir.' The aide pulled a bank of switches. 'Rotation accelerating, Sir. Point oh one to moon target, Sir. Sixty seconds to firing range. Sir … goodbye, Sir.' The aide saluted, putting the firing switch into Jerjerrod's hand as another explosion rocked the control room. Then he ran from the room.

Jerjerrod smiled calmly at the viewscreen. Endor was starting to emerge from the Death Star's eclipse. He fondled the detonation switch. Point oh oh five to moon target. Screams erupted in the next room.

Thirty seconds to firing time.

Lando was homing in on the reactor core shaft. Of the rest, only Wedge was left, flying just ahead of him, and Gold Wing just behind. Several TIE fighters still trailed them.

These central twistings were barely two planes wide, and turned sharply every few seconds. Another Imperial jet exploded against a wall: yet another shot down Gold Wing.

Now there were only two.

Lando's tail gunners kept the remaining TIE-fighters

jumping in the narrow space until, at last, the main reactor shaft came into view. Lando had never seen such an awesome reactor.

'It's too big, Gold Leader,' Wedge yelled. 'My proton torpedoes won't even dent it.'

'Go for the power regulator on the north tower,' Lando directed. 'I'll take the main reactor with concussion missiles. But we won't have much time to get out of here, once I let them go.'

He fired his torpedoes with a Corellian war cry, hitting both sides of the north tower, and peeled off, accelerating.

'I'm already on my way out,' Wedge exclaimed.

The *Falcon* waited three dangerous seconds. The flash was too bright to see the result at first. Then the whole reactor began to crumble.

'Direct hit!' shouted Lando. 'Now comes the hard part.'

The shaft was already caving in on him, creating a tunnel effect. The *Falcon* manoeuvred through the twisting outlet, through walls of flame, always only just ahead of the continuing chain of explosions.

Wedge tore out of the superstructure at barely sub-light speed, whipped round the near side of Endor, and coasted into deep space, slowing into a gentle arc to return to the safety of the moon.

A moment later Luke escaped the main docking bay in a destabilized Imperial shuttle. His wobbling craft too headed for the green sanctuary in the near distance.

Finally, as if being spat out of the very flames of hell, the *Millenium Falcon* shot towards Endor, only moments before the Death Star flared into brilliant oblivion.

As the Death Star exploded, Han was binding Leia's leg wound in a dell. Ewoks, stormtrooper prisoners and Rebel troops stood awe-stricken at this final turbulent flash of self-destruction. The Rebels cheered.

Han touched Leia's cheek. 'Don't worry,' he said encouragingly. 'I'll bet that Luke got off that thing before it blew up.'

That night a huge bonfire blazed in the centre of the Ewok village for the celebration. Rebels and Ewoks rejoiced in the warm firelight, singing, dancing, laughing.

Threepio, his days as a god in the village over, was content to sit near the little droid who was his best friend in the universe. He thanked the Maker that Captain Solo had been able to fix Artoo, not to mention Princess Leia. And he thanked the Maker that this bloody war was over.

Up there, somewhere, the Death Star had burned itself out.

Han, Leia and Chewbacca stood a short way from the revellers. They stayed close to each other, not talking. Periodically they glanced anxiously at the path that led to the village.

At last, their patience was rewarded. Luke and Lando, exhausted but happy, stumbled out of the darkness and into the light. Their friends rushed to greet them. They all embraced, cheered, slapped each other's backs. After a while, the two droids sidled over to stand with their dearest comrades.

While the small company of gallant adventurers looked on, the fuzzy Ewoks continued there cele- brations far into the night. Only Luke did not seem to feel the happiness the others shared.

He gazed silently into the forest, unable to forget the loss and the pain he had suffered that day. He still wondered if there was something different he could have done to help his father. He would always wonder. And, as long as he lived, he would never forget his father's face.

For a moment, looking into the bonfire, he thought he saw faces dancing – Yoda, Ben and … was it his father? He drew away from his companions, trying to see what the faces were saying, but they spoke only to the shadows of the flames, then disappeared completely.

Momentarily, Luke felt a wave of deep sadness. Then Leia took his hand and drew him back to the others, back to their circle of warmth, comradeship and love.

The Empire was dead.

Long live the Alliance.